PUPPY LOVE

After each returning from their gap years, Hannah and Ryan meet in the rural village where their parents live. Hannah is house-sitting for her family, and Ryan's mother and father have recently taken over The Seven Stars, a local inn. When pedigree dogs start to go missing locally, Hannah and Ryan — along with Hannah's grand-father — attempt to investigate the disappearances. As their amateur sleuth-ing brings the young couple closer together, will their partnership turn into something more . . . ?

JILL BARRY

PUPPY LOVE

Complete and Unabridged

LINFORD
Leicester

First published in Great Britain in 2015

First Linford Edition
published 2017

A catalogue record for this book is available
from the British Library.

ISBN 978–1–4448–3124–5

1

If a witch had transported her here, blindfolded, and asked her to identify her surroundings or else be transformed into a mouse, Hannah Ross would definitely not grow a long tail and start squeaking. She loved this part of Bailsford, and treasured happy memories of tranquil holidays spent in the village as a child and young teenager. Here, the sweet smell of jasmine was as unforgettable as the whiff of silage from the farm up the road.

Hannah wheeled her bicycle up the path and around the side of her grandfather's white-painted cottage. She loved houses with history, and always felt this was a dwelling holding many families' stories. It whispered of fun, banter, grief, joy and love. Mostly love. Whereas her parents' new house on the estate at the village's west end, although larger, swankier, and much more environmentally friendly, was still somewhere Hannah liked living in rather than loved.

She propped her bike against the shed and knocked on the cottage's back door. 'Granddad? It's me.' She let herself into the shabby, homely kitchen, calling out again. If she closed her eyes, she could imagine her grandma standing at the old Belfast sink, filling the kettle while chatting nineteen to the dozen about *The Great British Bake Off* contestants. Or litter louts. Or anything really.

'In here.' A voice floated through the open door leading to the hallway.

Hannah glanced around her before moving a step further. No dirty dishes in the sink. No crumbs on the worktop. 'Hey, Granddad,' she called. 'Haven't you had breakfast yet?'

She heard his familiar deep chuckle. 'You nag me worse than your mother does. Of course I have, and probably before you even got out of bed, young lady.'

She wandered into the sitting room and stood, hands on hips, wondering what kept her grandfather so focused upon his laptop.

'So, are you looking up family history or getting gloomy over the cricket score? Unless you've actually started on that book you keep talking about writing?'

'If you must know, I'm taking a look at our local paper's website.' Greg Ross peered over his spectacles at her. 'They've given some very good coverage to that family fun day the village hall committee organised. Come and see.'

'I just missed that, didn't I? But I won't recognise anyone, surely?'

'You might be surprised. Some of these folk have lived here for years and went to school with your dad. Lots of people know who you are, you can be sure of that, Hannah.'

She pulled up a chair. 'There's a pile

3

of newspapers back at the house.' She hesitated, watching her granddad raise his magnificent white eyebrows. 'Dad said I should read some back copies so I know what goes on in the village.'

'You don't sound too keen.'

'It's so weird, getting used to thinking of this being my home now. We lived in London. Bailsford was where we spent our holidays with you and Gran-Gran.'

'I know, sweetheart. But your father always wanted to come back here to live. I didn't think he'd opt for early retirement, but from a selfish point of view, it's lovely having you all so close, even if you'll be off to university come autumn.'

'I know how much you miss Gran-Gran. It's bad enough for us — it must be a thousand times worse for you.'

'Your grandmother would be a hard act to follow, that's for sure.'

'Granddad?'

'Oh, I didn't mean anything, lovey. I've a lot to be thankful for, and your

4

grandma made sure I knew my way around the washing machine and the cooker. Besides, who'd put up with an old curmudgeon like me?'

'I don't know what that means, but whatever it is, I'm sure you're not one.'

He laughed and pointed at the computer screen. 'That's a face you know, surely?'

'Of course. Debbie used to give me a jelly baby when I came into the shop with Mum or Gran-Gran.'

Her grandfather laughed. 'And now you're all grown up and back from your travels. Debbie's had a week off but she'll be working in the shop tomorrow. She's deputy housekeeper at the Manor House these days, mornings only, so she can do afternoon shifts in the stores.'

'So will you be showing me the ropes tomorrow, or will Debbie?'

'Both of us, I imagine. You can't do the Post Office counter, of course, not without proper training. But you'll be a great help with shelf-stocking and checking out shopping.'

'I hope I don't crash the till.'

'It's only a case of pressing the right buttons, but it took me a while to get used to this new system, believe me. I was fine with the old-fashioned sort where we just threw the money in the drawer.'

'I'm looking forward to helping. How many others work there besides you and Debbie?'

'There's a whole team of volunteers, plus Debbie as our manager. Didn't your mum tell you about it?'

'Not really. She and Dad couldn't wait to hear about my trip to Oz and New Zealand.'

'At least you returned in time to see each other before they set off.'

'My trip was booked ages before theirs, but they weren't to know how long it'd take to sell our house and buy one here.'

'Let's hope they enjoy their cruise.'

'They want to go out to Melbourne next January.'

'Following in your footsteps?'

'My carbon footprint, more likely.'

Her granddad groaned. 'Point taken. It's one heck of a long way from Bailsford, that's for sure.'

'I loved it. You should go one day, Granddad. See the other half of your family again. It was brilliant staying with Auntie Kate.'

'She wants to come over here when my youngest grandchild's a bit older. Meantime, we have our fortnightly Skype date.'

'You're very savvy, Gramps.'

He mock-punched her.

Hannah chuckled, well aware how he hated being called Gramps. She peered at the screen again. 'That looks fun. Was it a dog show?'

'It wasn't Crufts, that's for sure; but yes, it was fun. People had to turn up with their dog, do a twirl, and then wait for the vicar to decide which person most resembled his or her canine friend.'

'Did many people enter?'

'About ten.'

'I suppose there are lots of dogs in Bailsford.'

He smiled. Hannah spotted a faraway look in his eyes.

'You're thinking about Dougal, aren't you?'

'He had a good innings, as they say. Your grandmother used to think he and I resembled one another. Must've been the wild hairstyle!'

'And the eyebrows!' Hannah gave him a hug. 'Oh, it's good to have some time with you, Granddad. I hardly got to see you between moving house and going off again. The removal men had hardly drunk their mugs of tea and set off back to Sussex before Dad drove me to Heathrow.'

'It hasn't been the best of times as regards your settling into a new home, Hannah. I do understand how you must be feeling. It'll take time to adjust, especially after all your adventures.'

'Well, I've got masses of reading to do for my course. And Mum's planted shrubs and all kinds of flowers, so I have to keep everything from withering away.' She smiled at her grandfather. 'It's probably just as well Bailsford's such a peaceful place.'

★   ★   ★

Hannah knew her granddad always went to her folks' place for his Sunday meal, now they'd settled into their new abode. This weekend, he insisted she and he ate at The Seven Stars, only a short stroll from his cottage. When they arrived at the inn, he led the way to the restaurant entrance.

'We're nice and early,' he said. 'I reserved a table in the window for half-past twelve, so why don't we have a drink while we look at the menu?'

Hannah settled herself while her grandfather ordered a half-pint of lager plus her favourite, lime and soda. While she waited, she noticed several framed watercolours displayed on the walls, each with a price tag. From a distance, the pictures appeared to be beautiful paintings, mainly country scenes, some with figures grouped beside a lake or beneath trees. But these works weren't what she might have expected. Amongst the figures were some half-human, half-animal: their faces sprouting cat's whiskers, or their heads a spaniel's long ears. Fabulous interpretations of gnarled trees straight from an enchanted forest intrigued her so much, she got up to take a closer look.

She turned round as her granddad placed two tall glasses on the table. 'These are brilliant,' she said. 'They're all good, but the tree ones are really quirky. I keep finding twinkling eyes in the trunks, and birds or squirrels — even a snake or two — amongst the branches. I suppose they're by a local artist?'

'They're all young Ryan's handiwork. A bit far-fetched for my taste, but he's certainly talented.' Granddad held up his glass. 'Cheers, my dear. Here's to a happy future for you in Bailsford.'

'Thank you.' Hannah sat down. 'It's not like it's totally strange to me, is it? It's just such a contrast from life in London. That's why I always enjoyed coming here for holidays. Having the best of both worlds, I suppose.'

'I understand,' he said. 'You had an easy journey into the big city on the Tube; and apart from being close to good shops and theatres, you're bound to miss your friends.'

'That's one of the reasons I wanted to go travelling with my three best mates. But we're all off to different universities, so things would've changed anyway. And now Mum and Dad have moved here, I keep thinking of all the places I never got around to visiting. I can't believe all those different museums I didn't see.'

'That's always the way; and to be fair, London has a huge amount of sights to see. But you have time.' Her granddad's eyes twinkled. 'When you go to Bath, and you're not in lectures or studying, there'll be lots to see there.'

'I know. Can't wait to visit the Jane Austen Museum.'

'And Bath is, in fact, on a main railway line to London, don't forget!'

Hannah made a face at him.

'I'm sure those three friends of yours will invite you to stay in the holidays. And there's plenty of space in Number 11, Manor View if they fancy some country air.'

'That's true. Last time they came down, we camped in your garden. Do you remember that?'

'Of course. I'm not quite doolally yet,' he said.

'Sorry, Granddad! I still can't believe we have a downstairs cloakroom, a bathroom upstairs, and a master bedroom with en-suite fritillaries.' She grinned. 'Well, that's what Dad calls them, anyway.'

'Your father always had a wicked way with words. His puns are pretty excruciating, I must admit. Nothing changes.'

'I wonder where he gets that from!' Hannah sighed. 'I just hope he doesn't find retirement too boring.'

'I wouldn't worry about that happening. Your mum and dad both want to grow veggies for the local shop. And your dad's sent his CV to the Manor, in hopes of being invited to give a talk now and then.'

'Don't they have their own lecturers for those courses they run?'

'They do. But your father's knowledge of military history is impressive, so you never know, he may find he's sought after.'

'He could always lead a course on how to make puns.'

'Now, that's an excellent idea.'

'Good afternoon, Mr Ross. Are you ready to order now?'

Hannah looked up at the young man standing at her granddad's side. Dressed in dark trousers, a white open-neck shirt and striped apron, he looked smart and professional. His black hair was cropped short and he had a modest suntan. He gave her a quick glance, smiled, and returned his attention to her grandfather.

Wow. What a smile that was. Things were looking up if this boy was part of the local scenery. Surely he hadn't been one of the group she used to play with during those long, summer days? She certainly had no recollection of him being in the little gang she'd hung out with when they were all turning into teenagers.

There'd been games of tennis, picnics by the river, or just hanging out on the village green, discussing everything under the sun until, with the sun sinking below the horizon, they strolled back before the dreaded call came from someone's parents. She'd always hoped she wouldn't be the first to be reminded what the time was.

'I believe it's one roast beef and one chicken. Isn't that right, Hannah?'

Before she could answer, Granddad was apologising. 'I'm forgetting my manners. You two probably haven't met. Ryan, I'd like to introduce my granddaughter, Hannah. And Hannah, this is Ryan.'

'Surely *you* can't be Young Ryan?' At once Hannah felt heat flood her cheeks. Why did she always have to blush? Why couldn't she ever learn to think before she spoke?

'Sorry?'

'My fault, Ryan,' said Granddad cheerily. 'My granddaughter has been admiring your work. She wanted to know who the local artist was, and I referred to you as 'young Ryan'. Of course, to someone my age, you're both just fledglings.'

'Hi, Hannah,' said Ryan. 'I've met your parents a few times. It's good to meet you too.'

He was being polite. He must think she was a total nerd. Suddenly she realised he was holding out his hand, ready to shake hers. Her right hand shot out too, knocking over her glass.

'Oh, no,' she wailed. 'I'm so sorry.' An ice cube slid across the table and

15

landed in her lap. She longed to press it against her hot face.

Like a magician, Ryan produced a pristine white cloth and mopped the luckily-not-too-large puddle of lime and soda water forming on the table. With the other hand, he removed her glass.

'My fault,' he said. 'I wasn't paying enough attention. Let me replace your drink, Hannah, but first I'll put your lunch order into the kitchen.'

'There's no need for that, my boy,' said Granddad. 'Stick another couple of drinks on my tab.'

Ryan smiled. 'I wouldn't dream of it, sir.'

Hannah's eyes followed the young man as he walked back to the kitchen. Once he disappeared through the swing doors, she remembered she was sitting opposite her grandfather.

'Oh dear,' she said. 'How embarrassing was that?'

'Asking if he was Young Ryan, or knocking over your glass?'

'Both.'

'Fortunately, you'd drunk half of it. Fancy the boy, do you?'

'Granddad! What are you like?'

'I have a pair of eyes which function fairly well with the help of my specs. I still have a brain. And I have a beautiful granddaughter who's nineteen years old and who hasn't yet had time to make friends of her own age in this village.'

Hannah wished her cheeks would cool down. 'That doesn't mean I go round hoping to hit on guys, Granddad. Besides, he probably already has a girlfriend.' She didn't voice her opinion that Ryan was too gorgeous not to.

'I doubt he's found someone yet. He's not long returned from travelling, either. His parents only took over the pub at the beginning of the year. Father was in the Forces, and young Ryan attended boarding school for some years before he decided to join some kind of voluntary service scheme. I can't recall where it was, but he's off to university soon, like you are. And when he's not helping his folks, he paints. I

17

believe he sells quite a bit of his work.'

'I'm not surprised.' Hannah spotted Ryan returning with two glasses on a small tray. She placed both hands in her lap. Just in case.

'There we go. Your food's almost ready to serve, so you won't get rid of me for long, I'm afraid.'

Hannah gulped. Ryan set off again. Granddad winked at her. She glared back. There were occasions, she thought, when she forgot to behave like an adult.

*   *   *

Around seven o'clock that evening, Hannah, who'd long since changed from her pale green cotton frock into denim jeans and a lemon T-shirt, tied her long, black hair in a ponytail and headed outside to water the garden. June roses perfumed the air. Pinks chimed in, helped by lavender. Her mum's herb garden in a tub added scents of thyme and mint. It was a summer cocktail, and well worth the effort of filling watering cans from the outside tap.

'Can I give you a hand?'

It had to be him! Hannah turned round quickly. Ryan stood on the path behind their house's back fence, looking quizzically at her. He wore a pair of khaki cut-offs and a T-shirt bearing some kind of slogan, which she didn't dare try to read for fear he thought she was ogling him. He carried a small backpack.

'Don't you have to work tonight?'

He shook his head. 'No meals on a Sunday evening. Mum gets the night off too because the part-timer comes in. Dad's around, of course. We could finish the watering and go for a walk by the river. If you like.'

She told herself she should play it cool. But when did she ever use common sense? 'Okay. I'm up for that. If you like.'

His lips twitched. 'Do I vault over the fence, or is there an easier way?'

For once, her cheeks didn't burn up. 'Come round to the front and walk down the path at the side of the house.'

He joined her within moments, took the next watering can from her, and said, 'Shall I do the veggie garden?'

Before she knew it, they'd finished the chore.

'I need to lock up — and stuff,' she said.

'I'll wait for you by the gate.'

Thank goodness for the downstairs cloakroom! Hannah dashed inside, washed her hands, swiftly inspected her hair, pulled it loose from its band, brushed it, and let it hang free and glossy, not neglecting to fluff up the fringe more becomingly. She rushed back into the kitchen, where she picked up her lip-gloss from beside the microwave, hesitated, and put it down again. She didn't want to appear too keen, did she?

'You were quick,' he said when she reappeared. 'Did you think I might get bored waiting and run away?'

'No,' she said. 'I credit you with better manners than that. You were ace at lunchtime. Granddad thinks you're David Beckham and Andy Murray all rolled into one.'

'I wish. That's praise indeed because your grandfather is a top man. He knows about all kinds of stuff.'

They were walking away from the estate and towards the open countryside. She was doing what she'd been warned not to do, and that was going off with someone she'd only just met. Someone male. And, what was more, nobody in the world knew exactly where she was at that moment. She wouldn't have risked doing such a thing when she'd been travelling with her friends. They'd all made their personal security high priority. But this was sleepy Bailsford. And somehow, Ryan, even without her granddad's seal of approval, looked like the kind of guy you could trust.

2

They walked in single file along the track leading to the railway line. Masses of colourful flowers and shivery grass tumbled in the hedgerows, and the narrow footpath felt hard beneath Hannah's sandals. She almost walked into the back of Ryan when he stopped abruptly just before they reached the stile leading to the level crossing.

'Whoops!'

He turned to look at her. 'I'm sorry. Do you mind if I take some photographs?'

'Go ahead.' She watched Ryan capture clouds of wildflowers on his camera.

'Research?'

'Yeah, I might create a backdrop, kind of misty but with masses of blues, pinks and purples.'

'Impressionist-style.'

'Hopefully, but there'll be something totally unexpected hidden amongst the flowers.'

'Like some dolls' house furniture, or a toy train chugging along, maybe. I can imagine little woodland creatures sitting in the carriages.'

He stared at her, that fabulous smile lighting up his face and displaying even white teeth. Hannah's world turned upside down for a moment or three.

'You're interested in art?' He stood back so she could climb over the wooden stile.

'I took Art and Design as one of my A levels. I could never paint like you do, though.'

He landed beside her. 'Don't ever forget to check both ways before you cross here.'

'How many trains come through each day?'

He grinned. 'It'd only take one. Seriously, Hannah, we get four through each day, but sometimes a freight train will appear out of nowhere.'

'Thanks for the warning.'

He led the way across the track and over the stile on the other side. She fell into step with him as they headed across the field towards the riverbank. Hannah didn't have a clue what kind of birds she could hear trilling, but they made a lovely sound.

'Granddad used to tell me the names of all the birds singing when we came for walks down here. I never could remember which was which.'

'Your dad told me he was brought up here and always wanted to return. He also said he didn't think his daughter was too keen on the idea of leaving the city behind.'

'Did he now? I think I've always known my folks would end up living back here one day. I'm just grateful I'd already left school when it all started happening.'

'It must be a real culture shock, coming from London to Bailsford?'

'I was saying the same to my

granddad earlier, but I always loved spending holidays here, so it's cool really.'

'You and your grandfather seem close. I envy you that.' He stopped walking. 'Shall we sit? I brought a couple of cans with me.'

'I don't drink beer. Happy to sit down, though.'

'Contrary to popular opinion, not all pub landlords and their families actually drink the profits away.'

Whoops! He seemed a bit sensitive. Maybe he'd been teased?

He held out two cans. 'You choose. Guaranteed no alcohol.'

Hannah took one from him. It felt cool in her hand. 'I like this flavour.'

'Good. I brought two different sorts, just in case.'

She felt a little awkward, sitting beside him yet trying not to get too close. He'd chosen a spot near a weeping willow tree. She'd received her first kiss under that tree, probably five years ago now. She wondered whether the boy was still around, and hoped not.

'Chill, Hannah. I shan't try to kiss you or anything cringe-making like that.'

She felt her cheeks flood with warmth. 'I didn't want, I mean, I wasn't — ooh!' She roared with exasperation. 'You're the first guy I've talked to since I came back from the States, and I'm making such a hash of it. Sorry, Ryan. Again.'

'You're absolutely fine. I enjoy talking to you. You're the kind of person who — oh, now I'm the one making a hash of things.'

He looked sideways at her and they both burst out laughing.

'I'm a bit of a loner, Hannah. I'm not into Facebook and stuff like that. I don't hang out with the lads. I like playing tennis but apart from Dad, I haven't found anyone else here who'll have a game with me.'

'I love tennis.'

'Really? It would be great if we could

play some time. Dad enrolled me in the village club.'

'I noticed there are two courts on the sports ground now, but I haven't had a chance to join the club. What kind of people belong to it?'

'All kinds. Mums, dads and kids; some thirty-somethings, mostly from the estate where you live; and quite a few seniors. The other week, I played in a doubles match when someone dropped out.'

'Did your side win?'

'No way. Our opponents were annoyingly good. I hate losing.' He scowled.

A cool breeze stirred the leaves. Hannah watched the dog daisies dancing, and shivered too. 'Well, you won't have that problem if you challenge me to a singles match.'

'I might turn you into a tiger and paint you playing tennis with a kitten.'

'A tiger in a tennis dress?' She looked down and, seeing her arms were covered in goose pimples, hugged them around herself.

Ryan reached inside his rucksack and pulled out a black fleece. 'Here, put this on. We can go back when you want.'

'In a bit. It's lovely here, but I won't say no to the fleece.' She pulled it over her head. 'So, where did you live before your folks bought the pub?'

'It's not actually ours. They took over the lease, and Dad reckons, if all goes according to plan, they'll retire when the lease expires in ten years' time.'

'Ten years is a world away from now,' she said.

'I know. But that's how people their age think. Luckily they've really got a good thing going with the food and the real ale. We do barbecues at weekends, weather permitting.'

'You must be a great help to them.'

He shrugged. 'They don't expect me to muck in all the time, but it wouldn't suit me not to do my share. I'd rather wait on tables or help in the kitchen, though. Small talk isn't my strong point.'

'I know what you mean. If you don't

mind my saying, I find you very easy to talk to. Once we get going.' She looked sideways at him this time.

He went on staring at the river as it glided by on its way to meet up with another, bigger waterway. Hannah wondered if she'd embarrassed him.

'Yeah, well, that's something to be thankful for.' He collected their empty drinks cans and stuffed them into his rucksack. 'Would you mind if I took your photograph, Hannah?'

'What, here?'

'Wherever.'

'But why?'

'Do I have to give you a reason?' He pulled her to her feet, smiling, eyes dancing. Looking as if he hadn't a care in the world.

'Would you really put me in one of your watercolours?'

'If you'll let me.' He aimed his camera.

She started mucking about, deliberately posing like a publicity-hungry celebrity, tossing her long hair, waiting to see how he reacted.

He held up one hand. 'Can you hear that?'

She stood still and looked at him, chin tilted. 'Hear what?'

Ryan clicked and clicked again. 'Perfect.'

★ ★ ★

Back at the house, Ryan closed the front gate behind Hannah. She took off the fleece and held it out to him.

'Thanks.'

'No problem.' He moved back a step. 'I'll leave you to it, then. Are you sure you're okay, staying here on your own? At first I thought you were staying at Rose Cottage with your granddad.'

'I'm fine,' she said. 'I like my own space and it's a chance to get used to the house.'

'Good point. I hated moving from posting to posting when my father was in the Army. In the end, I asked if I could go to boarding school.'

'Really? How old were you?'

'Eleven. My parents chose one near Bournemouth, and I hated it at first, but it didn't turn out too bad. S'pose, if I'm honest, it kind of grounded me in more ways than one. That's where I began to take art seriously. Began to think of it as a career.'

'I love what I've seen of your work, but isn't there loads of competition?'

'I told you. I hate to lose. I want to be the best.'

'I'm wondering now why I agreed to give you a game of tennis.'

He leaned both his arms on the gate, bringing his head down more to her level. She didn't know she was going to do it until it happened. Hannah leaned forward and gave him a swift yet tender kiss on one cheek.

'I didn't mean to do that! I'm so sorry, Ryan. Again.'

At once, as if this was some kind of television soap drama, a van roared up the road and came to a stop opposite where the two stood. A head poked through the passenger window, causing Hannah to gasp with surprise.

'Flippin' heck, I wondered if it was you, and now I can see it is. Little Hannah Ross snogging in the open air! I thought you were still travelling with your mates. I'll never forget that summer you brought them down here to camp in your granddad's garden.'

Hannah opened her mouth to speak.

'Hey, who are you visiting, babes? This new estate's where the posh folk live.'

'I don't think so! My parents aren't posh, Ben.'

'Are you saying you live here now? Since when, babes? Caught up with any of the old gang yet?'

Hannah seethed. He was totally ignoring Ryan, and she could see her new friend clenching his fists. See his jaw set.

'You must be well out of touch. My folks moved here not long before I set off on my big adventure. So you haven't met Ryan then?'

Whoever was driving the vehicle gave a gurgle of laughter. Hannah didn't realise she'd said anything funny. She looked at the driver for the first time, and saw a pale-faced young man wearing a hooded top very like the one she'd just handed back to Ryan. Ben's mate had that designer stubble look so many young guys seemed to copy. He hadn't pulled the hood up but kept his head down, showing brown hair tied back in a ponytail. He kept his gaze focused on his mobile phone. Music boomed from the speakers. No wonder Ben was shouting.

Ben nodded. 'I know who Ryan is. So what are you doing with yourself, babes?'

'This and that. I have to go now. Stuff to do.'

'If you say so.' At last Ben turned his attention to Ryan. 'Want a lift back to your place? That's where we're heading. You wouldn't want to keep Hannah from her studying, now, would you?'

'I'm good, thanks. I enjoy walking.'

Ryan stood his ground.

'See you around then, dude. Catch you soon, Hannah. Maybe underneath that old willow tree. Happy memories, eh, babes?'

He turned to address his driver. 'Let's go! You can buy me a pint while I chat up that new barmaid.'

Hannah watched as the van travelled to the end of the road, drove into the hammerhead to turn, and accelerated past them. She waited until it joined the road to the village centre and made a wry face at Ryan.

'Sorry about that. He's okay, really, is Ben. I was never his girlfriend, if that's what you're wondering.'

Ryan's face was grim. 'Whatever. The thing is, Hannah, I saw that van earlier, parked outside one of the old farm workers' cottages opposite the green.'

'That's where Ben lives. Where his mum and dad live, I should say. Ben works in Bristol, so he rents a flat there. I only know because Granddad's been catching me up on the local gossip.'

She thought Ryan looked relieved for a moment before his guard swiftly shot up again.

'I don't know who lives where, but I noticed the vehicle because it's so scruffy. You couldn't fail to recognise it, could you?'

'It could do with a wash and polish, but I suppose those mauve stripes running across it make it quite distinctive.'

'When I was in the beer garden this morning, making sure everything was tidy, I noticed that van parked by the rank of cottages.'

'I can't see anything strange about that. Maybe Ben's mate offered to drive him to Bailsford for the day. They probably had Sunday dins with Ben's parents, and now they're on their way back to Bristol. Ben works in a call centre, so I guess he'd have to be back for Monday morning.'

'I saw it again, parked near the vicarage, when I came out this evening to call on you.'

'Yeah, how did you know which house was ours? Please don't tell me Granddad informed you!'

Ryan grinned. 'He did, actually. Told you he was a top man.'

She groaned. 'I am so mortified. Apologies, Ryan. Mr Gregory Ross is a sweetheart, but he's a bit of a busybody at times.'

'Well, maybe he and I have something in common. So tell me why those two guys would be visiting the vicarage.'

Hannah gave it thought. 'Perhaps Ben's friend is considering becoming a clergyman. You should never judge a person by their appearance,' she said sternly.

'Maybe not, but I think you're having a laugh. And I still think it's bizarre how they were driving down Manor View for no particular purpose.'

'Ben heard I was back and wanted to catch up?'

'Come on, Hannah. You heard how surprised he was to see you. He didn't know your folks had bought a place here, that's for sure.'

She didn't like to say her mind had been on other things when the scruffy white van pulled up and shattered the mood, not to mention the eardrums of anyone unfortunate enough to be nearby.

'And another thing — why on earth would they want to visit the pub after leaving here, when Ben lives opposite us and they've had all day to drop in?'

'Perhaps he fancied a pint of your dad's guest ale? I agree the tough-looking guy wouldn't be able to drink 'cause he's driving, but — oh, I don't know, Ryan. Why do you still look so stressed? They're going back to Bristol, so if you're concerned about them coming back here, it's very sweet of you, but I really don't think there's a problem.'

He took out his mobile phone. 'Humour me, Hannah. Will you give me your number, please? And if it's all right with you, I'd like you to have mine.'

'Well, okay, if that's what you want.'

'You can't blame a guy for wanting to take your phone number!'

Hannah shook her head at him. 'It's nice of you to want to keep an eye on me. I suppose I could text you later.'

'Please. I'll look forward to it.'

She watched him smile again. She loved his smile. Seeing it had the same effect as getting home to find your mum had made a big squidgy chocolate cake. She couldn't help thinking he was overreacting, but exchanging phone numbers was something friends did. And she thought they were certainly friends.

'Be sure to bolt the doors once you're inside,' he said.

⋆   ⋆   ⋆

Ryan walked back in a thoughtful mood. He hoped he hadn't put Hannah off. Especially as he didn't exactly have a big bunch of friends to hang out with. Nor had he ever. The last thing he'd expected to find in this village was a friend. Especially not a girlfriend — a proper girlfriend who'd hold his hand and hug him and make him wonder how he'd cope without her when they both went away to uni. But that exciting possibility wouldn't leave his mind now. And it was all down to Mr Gregory Ross. Sort of.

Ryan had noticed Hannah immediately she walked into his parents' pub with her granddad. He'd have to have been some kind of android not to be hit for six. Those lovely brown eyes looking up at him when he arrived to take the order. That long black hair she tied back when she was doing stuff like gardening. He had never, ever been brave enough to turn up at a girl's house as he'd done earlier. And when she agreed to go for a walk, and he caught a drift of her shampoo as they sat on the riverbank . . . he could still smell the sweet, clean fragrance of coconut.

But maybe she'd felt sorry for him,

turning up like a lost soul. By now, she'd be wondering whether he had a phobia about strangers. He'd probably ranted too much about Ben and his oddball mate. Worst of all, he'd blurted out that comment about having something in common with Hannah's grandfather. Yeah, right; Ryan, the geriatric young adult. He sighed. He'd spent too much time on his own. Even now, he was keeping an eye open for that van. He really wouldn't put it past Ben to get his mate to drive him back to Hannah's place.

He didn't really think they meant her any harm. He knew how young men liked to show off in front of their friends, especially when there were girls around. Ben and Hannah had known one another several years. He, Ryan, was the incomer. Not Ben. And Hannah had been spending time in the village probably since she was a toddler.

But there had been that kiss when he'd stood outside her gate. Right out of nowhere. He'd longed for that to happen when they sat under that tree. But if he'd kissed her first, that would've been out of order. So what if it had only been a kiss on the cheek? It was still a kiss, meaning she couldn't think he was too weird, surely?

Now he was within sight of The Seven Stars, its distinctive gold and azure pub sign swaying gently in the breeze. Ryan hurried down the road. There was only one vehicle parked outside the rank of cottages and that was a green Mini. He headed towards the car park and saw six or seven vehicles. Not bad for a Sunday night. He saw no sign of the one he was looking for amongst them, so checked out the overflow parking area. Not one vehicle, apart from his father's estate car and the little saloon his mum let him borrow. She'd said he could use it when he started at uni.

He let himself in through the kitchen door, suddenly ravenous. There was a fully-fitted kitchenette in the family apartment upstairs, but Ryan fancied checking for leftovers. His mum's cooking was great, and normally plates were scraped clean and vegetable dishes returned empty, but it was worth having a look.

He wolfed two still-crispy roast potatoes and a succulent wedge of Yorkshire pudding. Guiltily, he hoped no one else had been contemplating a late-evening snack. He opened the door to the public bar and checked the barmaid was coping okay. She told him his father had come down for an hour, but she was fine for now.

He headed upstairs to say goodnight, and found his mum making hot drinks and his dad watching an action movie in their sitting room.

'Dad,' he said, 'when you were in the bar, did you notice a couple of young guys? The parents of one of them live across the way, but the other's a stranger, I think.'

His father paused the film. 'Ben Abbott was in, throwing his weight around — or trying to. Kelly's great at polite brush-offs. Such a good skill for someone working behind a bar.'

Ryan waited patiently.

'So, um, Ben came in with a quiet young man, who I'd describe as having an almost-beard and long brown hair tied back in a ponytail.'

Ryan nodded. 'That sounds about right.'

'A Diet Coke and a pint of lager. They didn't hang around for long after Ben failed to chat up Kelly, but they spent some time reading the notice-board.'

'That's more than I've done.'

'You haven't missed much, son. Let me think.' His dad ticked off items on his fingers. 'WI jumble sale. A couple of adverts for a dog walker. There's a reminder about the flower and produce show later this month, and a card offering two puppies for sale. They're one of those posh breeds, and your mum's tempted to buy one, but I'm not so sure.'

'Can you remember who's advertising the puppies?'

'Um, the vicar, I think. Why? Do you know someone who's interested?'

3

'Granddad, how long have you been here?' Hannah walked into the local stores to find him seated behind the till.

'Ages!' Greg Ross's eyes twinkled. 'Good morning, darling, you're not late. Someone has to be here at half-seven ready for the newspaper and magazine delivery. One of the village youngsters delivers to the old people's bungalows, so that's an important task sorted. From the next hour or so, you'll find people calling in for a paper and small items, like chocolate or fruit, on their way to work.'

'What would you like me to do?'

'I'll give you a tour so you know the stockroom layout and where the tea-making station is — most important. Maybe you'd like to check out the shelves in case a new customer comes in and asks where to find the baked beans.'

'What about teaching me how to use the till, and how to deal with debit and credit cards? Do you take them?'

'We do. All will be revealed.'

The hours sped by. Hannah observed, and was given the job of checking that greengrocery and chill cabinet produce was up to standard. She learnt about sell-by dates, and when Debbie arrived to take over from Greg, Hannah had already checked out a few customers' goods.

'You're a sight for sore eyes,' said Debbie. 'Mornin', Greg. Lovely to see your Hannah again.' She beamed at them both.

'Luckily, she's a fast learner. So, how was the holiday?'

'Wonderful. Could've done with another week, but there you go. Anything to report?'

'Village scandal or trading patterns?' Granddad peered over his specs at her.

Debbie looked at Hannah. 'Has he

46

been at the sherbet lemons?'

'I try my best to keep an eye on him,' said Hannah.

'I can see whose side you're on.' But Granddad was smiling. 'Things much as usual, Debbie, you'll be pleased to hear. Now, I'll sign myself out and take this young lady for a ploughman's.' He turned to Hannah. 'Maybe you'd like to come back afterwards and spend an hour or so with Debbie so she can see how much you've learnt.'

'Okay,' said Hannah. She couldn't help wondering whether Ryan would be on duty again. 'Catch you later, Debbie.'

She followed her granddad out. 'She looks just the same as I remember her, but surely that can't be possible?'

'When you never saw someone grow from baby to adult, I think you probably always remember them looking the same. We oldies have clear recollections of how our children and grandchildren looked as babies. I remember Debbie from her childhood days, singing in the church choir and dredging her fishing net in the pond, hoping to catch some unfortunate minnow.'

Hannah chuckled. 'I remember doing that. We always threw them back, but the poor little things were probably traumatised.'

They walked in silence until they reached The Seven Stars. Hannah noticed a few cars in the car park and wondered whether Ryan had passed his test. Her driving lessons had been put on hold, as she and her friends had decided to take off and see as much of other countries as they could before settling down to a tough three years of studying.

'We'll go into the restaurant side; and if it's quiet, we can sit at the bar, and you can meet Mike Hawkins.'

Granddad greeted the landlord smiling at them from behind the shiny taps of the drinks dispensers.

'We don't often see you on a Monday lunchtime, Mr Ross. Your usual, is it?

48

And how about this young lady?' He smiled at Hannah. 'Your granddad's one of this village's shining lights — but I imagine you know that.'

'I do. He's training me so I can help in the store.' Hannah knew that, thanks to the local community jungle drums, everyone in the pub yesterday would have known she was Greg Ross's granddaughter, back to look after the family home after months of travelling.

'Great stuff. I can't very well ask Ryan to do a shift too, as he's helping us out here until he goes to uni.'

Hannah looked towards the swing door leading to the kitchen.

'He's gone out with his camera,' said Mr Hawkins. 'Did you take a look at his paintings when you were in yesterday?'

Hannah knew her cheeks were turning rosy. She focused on the landlord's deft movements as he poured lemonade over ice cubes and measured lager into a half-pint glass. 'They're awesome. I wish I could do stuff like that. I'm more into bright colours and

49

geometric shapes, but I've fallen in love with Ryan's work.'

She willed her grandfather not to embarrass her. Fortunately he was checking the menu.

'I reckon a bacon sarnie would go down well,' he said. 'To me, a baguette will always be a sarnie. How about you, love?'

'Just an ordinary ploughman's will be great. Can I get it with wholemeal bread, please?'

Ryan's dad placed a perfect froth-topped glass of lager before her grandfather. 'I'll take your orders through. My wife's on her own in the kitchen as Mondays are usually quiet.' He disappeared through the swing door.

'Pleasant fellow. Never talks about his Army service, but I imagine he has many interesting stories to tell. Not that I'd try to find out. He's very clued up about cricket, so we can bore one another for hours given the chance.'

Mike Hawkins reappeared. 'Did

someone mention that fine game with bat and ball?'

Hannah squealed. 'Please, no. No. No.'

The two men laughed.

'My son's not too bad a batsman, as your grandfather knows. According to Ryan's school reports, he was torn between that and tennis.'

Hannah suspected Ryan would curl up with embarrassment if he could hear this.

'Do you play tennis, Hannah?'

'She was in her school team,' said Granddad proudly.

'Only just,' she said.

'And she's an Andy Murray fan.' Granddad winked at the landlord.

'Maybe you and my son can play together some time,' said Mike Hawkins. 'Wednesday is club night at the courts. You should go along, Hannah. Show 'em a thing or two.'

She reached for her glass and took a sip. 'I'm a bit rusty. Maybe I'll pass on that 'til I've got my eye in again.'

'The vicar's daughter plays. She must be about your age. She and Ryan were seeing each other for a while, but it didn't last long. Well, I don't think so, anyway. You never know with my son.'

Hannah remembered the girl from the vicarage as being hot on the tennis court, but a bit too sporty for her liking. She wouldn't be surprised to find Jodie was planning to train as a PE teacher or something similar at uni. As for Mr Hawkins's last comment, she wondered if he meant it as some kind of warning.

* * *

The days meandered by like the river running near the railway line, yet not quite so lazily. Hannah's garden-watering duties stopped temporarily as the weather took a turn for the worse. Her grandfather picked up a summer cold, but insisted he was quite able to do his usual shifts at the stores — until both Hannah and Debbie, each equally as stubborn as Greg, ordered him to stay home and not risk spreading germs amongst customers.

'Sorted,' said Hannah as she turned up for one of her morning shifts. 'I called round to make his porridge, and he was still in bed but promised he'd be up and in the shower soon. He says he's had enough of being an invalid, but he won't come back until he has permission from his two gaolers!'

'That sounds like Greg. I'm glad he has you around to keep tabs on him while your folks are away.' Debbie paused. 'Okay, I'm going to hide in the back, and you can deal with this next lot on your own. I think you've been coping well for days now, but this is kind of like your official inspection before we take off your stabilisers.'

'No pressure, then!' Hannah knew the older woman had rearranged her hours at the Manor House in order to ensure her new helper could safely be left in charge of the village shop.

Hannah checked out a packet of spaghetti, some fresh vegetables and a celebrity magazine for a woman she hadn't seen before. A couple of men came through the door behind the woman, but their purchases were daily papers; and, in one case, cough sweets. Hannah hoped there wasn't some sort of lurgy going around. At least her grandfather had seen sense and put his feet up while he felt poorly.

When she'd commiserated with the hoarse-voiced customer and discussed the merits of the medicated lozenges the shop stocked, she was alone again, and Debbie came through. 'You're doing a grand job. Now, what if someone wants to pay with a debit or credit card? You're sure you can cope?'

'Granddad used his credit card to pay his paper bill on my first day,' said Hannah. 'And two people, including the vicar's wife, did the same yesterday. So I've had a go, and I've made a note of what to do, in case I forget.'

Debbie laughed. 'I doubt you'll do that. Sounds like you'll be fine; but if there does happen to be a problem, you'll have to use your own judgement or try my mobile number. Not to mention, ring your granddad now he's perking up again.'

'Thanks, Debbie. Am I allowed to restock items? We could do with some more chocolate digestives on the shelf.'

'Good thinking, Batman. If you take anything from the stock room into the shop, remember to write it down on the list.'

'I know the one you mean.'

'And if our stocks of anything are running low, be sure to point it out to the person taking over from you. That'll often be me.'

'Okay. It's probably my granddad running down the biscuit stock. I don't know how he doesn't put on weight.'

Debbie went to get her raincoat. 'To be fair, he's a very active gentleman,' she said over her shoulder.

Hannah looked up as the door opened.

'Good morning.' A grey-haired woman,

wearing a dark red mackintosh, approached the counter.

She looks, thought Hannah, *as if she's received bad news*. 'Hi,' she said, trying not to sound too cheerful. 'Do you need any help?'

'Oh, my dear . . . ' The woman reached into a shopping bag and produced a homemade poster, protected by a plastic wallet. 'Could I ask you to put this up for me? We're going frantic with worry.'

Hannah looked at the poster and gasped. The poster showed the picture of a dog. Large letters proclaimed:

LOST DOG —
ANSWERS TO THE NAME OF
TOFFEE — MISSING FROM HER
HOME AT GREEN VIEW — IF
YOU SEE HER, PLEASE RING . . .

Debbie came out of the stockroom.

'This poor lady's dog is missing,' said Hannah. 'Is it okay to put the poster in the window?'

'Of course. Shall I leave that to you?' Debbie turned to their customer. 'I'm so sorry, Mrs Andrews. How long has Toffee been gone?'

'Since yesterday evening. We went out to the cinema, and left her in the utility room as we always do.' Mrs Andrews gulped. 'Her bed and her toys are in there. Toffee likes the radio, so I always leave it on. But if we plan on being out for more than a few hours, the boy next door calls round and lets her into the garden.' She looked wistful. 'He loves playing with her, and he always makes sure there's plenty of water in her bowl.'

'But I suppose if you were only going out for a few hours last night, you didn't need to call on the lad next door?'

'That's right. We go into town most Wednesday evenings. Who'd ever imagine such a horrible thing as this could happen? The moment we got home, I went in through the back door to see Toffee, just as I always do while my husband locks up the garage — but this time there was no sign of her. We searched the garden and called her for ages. My husband drove around, but of course it was dark by then, and — oh, dear — I'm so worried.'

'So, someone definitely broke into your house?'

Mrs Andrews bit her lip. 'We've got in the habit of locking the connecting door to the kitchen and leaving the door to the yard unlocked. There's nothing in the utility room worth stealing, unless thieves want to disconnect the washing machine or walk off with my rickety ironing board.'

'It sounds as if someone found Toffee worth stealing.' Debbie spoke gently. 'Have you contacted the police, Mrs Andrews?'

'I rang them earlier, but I had to confess we left the back door unlocked. They took the details, but do you really think the police want to be bothered with a lost dog?'

Hannah exchanged glances with Debbie. 'If you like, I can put something on social media, unless you'd prefer to do that yourself. I can also find out from the council if their dog wardens have picked up an animal answering to Toffee's description.'

'Oh, would you really do all that for us? Thank you so much. We have a computer, but we use it mostly for emailing our family.'

'I think there's enough information on your poster, so I'll make a photocopy before I stick it in the window. As soon as I get home, I'll go online. I imagine loads of people will help spread the word.'

'Goodness.' Mrs Andrews delved into her handbag. 'If it helps, would you like to borrow this photo?'

'Brilliant. I'll use my dad's computer and scan it in. He's got all the kit.' Hannah looked down at the photograph and studied it. 'Wow, what a cute little dog. We just have to get her back to you.'

★ ★ ★

Having handed over her shop duties to Debbie, the only paid staff member, Hannah set off home and looked up the number of the council department she needed. With no success from this, she quickly found a Facebook page dedicated to Dogs Lost and Found in the county. Hannah worded what she thought was an eye-catching appeal for help, and uploaded the photo of Toffee she'd borrowed from Mrs Andrews. She added some tags, ensuring that people who regularly helped send information winging round would be alerted.

As soon as she could, she set off on her bicycle to her grandfather's, stopping on the way to ask Ryan's dad if he would put a poster up in the pub.

'I'm pleased to help,' said Mike Hawkins. 'I don't know these people, but plenty of dog lovers come in here, so let's keep our fingers crossed.'

Hannah thanked him and turned to leave, but her attention was caught when the kitchen door opened and Ryan came into the bar.

'I'm off now, Dad.'

'Thanks, son. Look who you almost missed!'

Hannah saw Ryan's cheeks turn pink. No way! She was usually the one who blushed. 'Hi, Ryan. I'm helping spread the word about a dog theft. Your dad's kindly agreed to put up a poster — it'd be a great help if you could keep an eye open for Toffee while you're out.'

Ryan peered at the poster while he shrugged on his leather jacket. 'If you fancy some company, I'm off for a walk now the rain's stopped. I'm hoping to find some good puddles.'

His father chuckled. 'Chat-up line of the week! How could any young lady resist a tempting offer like that?'

'Just ignore him, Hannah. See you, Dad.'

Ryan followed her into the pub car park.

She grabbed her bike and began wheeling it. 'I'm off to see my granddad, but you're welcome to come too.'

'Cheers, but I really need to take these photos.' He paused. 'Um, they have a pop-up café at the Manor House all through the summer. Do you fancy meeting me there, about four o'clock?'

'I'd like that.' This time she did feel a blush coming on. Typical.

'How are you getting on at the shop?'

'They trusted me to be left in total charge this morning. Can't believe it. Luckily, I didn't jam the till, or get asked for anything I couldn't find. It's good fun.'

'I bet you loved playing shops when you were little.'

'I did. And Post Offices. But the one in the shop is manned certain hours a week, and obviously I'm not trained for that.'

'Just as well. Didn't you say you had uni stuff to do, apart from the watering?'

'Lots of reading for my course, yes. How about you?'

'Yep. These photographs are partly to

do with my course, partly for my paintings.'

'It's good to have plenty to do when you live somewhere with no distractions. It still seems weird to me, having no big stores and supermarkets close handy.'

He didn't reply. They walked in silence for a while until Hannah pointed to a gap in the hedgerow.

'I go through there. It's a shortcut to Rose Cottage.'

'Okay.' He nodded. 'Catch you later.'

'Happy puddle-hunting,' she called.

Ryan turned round. Did he realise, wondered Hannah, just how devastating he was once he lost that dark, brooding look? That smile, when he found it, was worth a thousand rainbows.

She wheeled her bike through the gap, giving a little huff of annoyance to find herself forced to walk through a puddle the size of Loch Ness. If only Ryan had accompanied her to Rose Cottage, he'd have been sure to photograph it. She must tip him off later, because it was unlikely that particular pool of water would evaporate in a hurry.

4

Bailsford Manor House sat in solitary splendour at the edge of the village. The magnificent building, constructed from Cotswold stone, loomed into view as Hannah rounded the curve in the driveway. On the lawn, a gardener was engrossed in his task of deadheading roses, and she recognised him as a friend of her granddad's as well as official scorer for the cricket team. She called out rather than suddenly creep up on him.

'Hello there! It's me, Hannah.' She didn't see any *Keep Off the Grass* notices, so walked across the velvety turf. 'I'm sorry to disturb you, Mr Crane, but I'm helping someone locate a lost pet. Have you by any chance seen a pretty, toffee-coloured dog? She's a Petit Basset, if that means anything to you.'

The gardener pulled off his battered sunhat and scratched his head. 'Sounds posh, don't it? Can't help, ducks, I'm afraid. But I'll keep my eye open. Wandered off, did her? I expect the little 'un will turn up again when her starts missing her home comforts. They usually does.'

'Sadly, it seems someone took her from her home. Mr and Mrs Andrews from Green View are the owners.'

Mr Crane nodded. 'I know who you mean. Theirs is the cottage tucked away beyond the vicarage. Keep themselves to themselves, they do. Reckon they must be gutted. Let's hope their dog's not been carted off miles from nowhere.'

Hannah stared at him. Somehow she hadn't pictured anyone driving Toffee out of the county to who-knew-where.

'It happens, you know. Anyway, good luck, my maid. I'll keep an eye open in case she wanders in here. Don't forget to tell your granddad I hope he'll be fit enough to ride on the coach come

Saturday. We've got an away match, and we could do with some support. I don't suppose you'd like — '

'Um, no, sorry. I've got loads to do, what with working in the shop and looking after our house.' She thought of her book pile and felt a pang of guilt. 'But I'll remind Granddad. He seems a lot better today, and I doubt he'll miss the cricket if he can help it.'

The gardener raised his hand to greet someone else. Hannah turned around to see Ryan striding towards them.

'Ah,' said Mr Crane, giving Hannah a knowing look. 'Tea for two, is it? You and the landlord's boy must be about the same age. Now, he's no slouch when it comes to wielding a cricket bat, if he weren't forever mooning about and doing all that painting he's so keen on.'

Hannah didn't only blush; she feared her cheeks were turning scarlet. She'd mentioned how busy she was, and promptly been caught out. Such was village life. You either loved it or couldn't wait to escape it.

Hannah and Ryan followed signs leading them along an arched walkway draped with climbing roses and down a path to the orangery. Hannah saw about a dozen tables, and a makeshift but practical counter displaying home-made cakes and cookies beneath glass domes. A couple of women wearing green-and-white aprons and caps were in charge. Despite it being a weekday, little groups of people, including a couple of young mums with toddlers, were chatting and enjoying refreshments. The smell of good coffee blended with the scent of sweet-smelling honeysuckle and roses.

'Do you want to grab that table by the window? What would you like to drink?'

'Lemonade please, Ryan.'

'I'll get cake too. I need cake. You up for that?'

Hannah was about to opt for a polite refusal when she spotted a towering creation, its four layers spread with thick coffee buttercream, the top one showered with shavings of dark chocolate.

'Oh, just look at that. To die for.'

'Yeah. Death By Chocolate Cake for two, then.'

She laughed. 'Followed by a game of tennis?'

'I'm up for it, if you insist.'

'Maybe when the weather improves!'

'I'll hold you to that,' he said, heading for the counter.

She walked across to the window and gazed up at the antiquated but decorative light fittings. The conservatory, with its glazed roof panes and walls with tall, elegant glass panels, must once have housed exotic plants, and Hannah suspected that was a young grapevine she could see at one end. The people who took over the manor house had converted it into a conference and educational centre with its own catering arrangements. The owners were probably seeing how this temporary tearoom fared before they took on the expense of fitting out a permanent restaurant.

She wondered whether it was worth her while to ask people enjoying their teas if they'd seen any sign of the missing dog, but decided against it. If, as Mrs Andrews said, little Toffee had been tucked away in the utility room before her master and mistress drove off to see a film, no one could possibly have seen her. If only the boy next door had been asked to call, he might have surprised the dog thief. But then, he might have been hurt, depending on how aggressive the thief had been, and that didn't bear thinking about.

Hannah frowned, struggling to get her head round the puzzle. Alarm bells were ringing — but if she wasn't careful, she'd be guilty of what she'd accused Ryan of when he started questioning what Ben and his friend were doing, driving round a part of the village where they didn't need to be.

She watched the tall young man pay at the till. He picked up the tray and headed for her table.

'Please let me pay for my share,' she said.

'No way. My treat.'

Ryan placed a portion of luscious cake in front of her and handed her a bottle of lemonade topped with an upside-down tumbler. She poured half the liquid into the glass. He had a mug of tea in front him. They picked up their forks at the same time.

'I'm looking forward to this.' Ryan bit into his cake and munched contentedly. 'Wow, hope you're not counting calories, Hannah.'

She took a more ladylike mouthful. 'Mmm, this is much too delicious to worry about calories. I must look on the Manor's website and see if they show the recipe. I could make this as a welcome-home surprise for Mum and Dad.'

'How long are they away on the cruise?'

'Ages yet. I might have to do a trial bake first.'

'Well, count me in if you need a guinea pig to practise on.'

They locked gazes and Hannah felt a little swirl of delight flutter deep in her tummy. Something she hadn't experienced since she developed a huge crush on a boy from Sydney who'd hung out with Hannah and her friends for a couple of days while they were wandering around the area. The boy had asked her out on the girls' last night in the city and they'd shared a cartwheel pizza and enjoyed one another's company but he hadn't suggested keeping in touch — and she'd decided it was probably just as well, with her new life about to unfold.

She couldn't even remember what colour eyes her Aussie date had had. Ryan's were dark brown and, like so many men, he possessed amazingly long, thick eyelashes, whereas Hannah used a little mascara to give hers more oomph.

'Your eyes are an amazing colour,' he said, catching her unawares. 'That shade of blue has to be periwinkle.'

'I always think that's a silly name for a flower,' she said, knowing she was dealing awkwardly with his compliment.

He concentrated on digging into his cake.

'Ryan, do you mind if I run something by you?'

'Feel free. But if it's about me turning up for cricket practice, thanks but no thanks.'

'Why would I try to force you into doing something you obviously don't want to do?'

He muttered something that she thought sounded very much like 'girls' being 'scheming and bossy'.

'If you meant me to hear that,' she said sternly, 'the amount of cake you had in your mouth turned your remark into total gibberish. Who's rattled your cage, Ryan?'

He reached across and gently dabbed

73

her nose with his paper napkin.

'Oh, gross,' said Hannah.

To her dismay, he looked stricken.

'I'm sorry,' he said. 'I didn't think you'd want anyone to notice that smudge of chocolate.'

'I d-didn't mean you were gross. I meant me was. I was. Oh, I give up!'

They locked gazes and laughter came easily.

'Shall we start again?'

She nodded. If she tried really hard, she could act like someone hoping to teach five-year-olds rather than act like one of them. But wasn't it partly Ryan's fault for sending mixed messages? What was more, she was cross with herself for starting to fall in love with him.

'Right,' she said. 'Last Sunday evening, outside my house? You remember how I thought you were too quick to think the worst when you were puzzling over Ben and his friend driving past.'

'Uh-huh. I still can't understand why they'd turn into the close.'

'I didn't think anything more of it until this afternoon when I told the gardener about Mrs Andrews having her dog stolen. Mr Crane said she and her husband live close by the vicarage.'

'Is that right? I don't think they ever come into the pub, so I haven't a clue who they are.'

'Too much chocolate cake doth clog the brain!' Hannah leaned forward. 'What did you say to me about that old white van Ben's mate was driving?'

Ryan took a gulp of tea. 'Um, I couldn't fathom why they were driving down your road, if they were on their way back to Bristol.'

'And what else?'

He thought for a few moments. 'I'd seen that same vehicle parked near the vicarage earlier. Remember you suggested Ben's mate maybe wanted to become a priest or whatever?'

Hannah nodded, and nibbled another delicious morsel of mocha-flavoured heavenliness.

Ryan's black brows drew together.

'Are you saying those guys were calling on Mrs Andrews?'

'Not in the way you mean. What if they were casing the joint?'

'With the intention of nicking stuff?'

'Think about it.'

He smacked his forehead. 'I've caught up with you at last. Sorry, Hannah. You're putting two and two together to make five now?'

'Or even four.'

He put down his spoon. 'Does the name Collinswood ring any bells?'

'I don't think so. Why?'

'Your granddad would know it because Bailsford cricket team play in the same league as Collinswood. Not long after we moved here, in a mad moment I agreed to be in the team. They were short of players and my dad dropped me in it.'

'He is a parent, don't forget.'

'Yeah. What I'm trying to say is, the captain of the Collinswood team came back with everyone after the match and had a drink or two. Mum had already hung some of my watercolours in the bar and this man wanted to know who'd painted them. I got dragged over to talk to him, and he told me he'd had his dog stolen a few months before.'

Hannah waited, not sure where this was going.

'The guy asked if he could email me some photos in hopes that I could paint a portrait of, um, Digby. Yeah, Digby was the name.'

'So, did poor Digby ever get found?'

'No, but the cricket captain told me there'd been several dog thefts in and around Collinswood. The last he saw of Digby was when he went to see what he was up to and found him snoozing under a bush in the front garden. The dog seemed quite happy so the guy went into the house to have his lunch. They had guests, so he didn't go back out for an hour or so, then he suddenly realised Digby hadn't wandered back in through the kitchen door like he usually did.'

'And there was no sign of him in the garden?'

'Or anywhere. They searched all round the outside and in the house in case he'd come in unnoticed and gone upstairs. No luck. After the police were alerted, it became clear these thefts were becoming regular. Every sign of it being a gang, according to the cops.'

'A gang of dognappers?'

'Not necessarily. The cricket captain didn't think anyone had been asked to pay a ransom. It's possible those dogs were whisked away by dog thieves, driven to the other side of the country, and sold for a nice fat sum.'

'How awful. Do you really think Toffee's the victim of something similar?'

'I hate to say this, Hannah, but unless Mr and Mrs Andrews receive a ransom note, it seems likely their pet will be changing hands, never to be seen in these parts again.'

'But how do these thieves get away with it? Wouldn't the animals bark and kick up a fuss if they were bundled into a car boot?'

'Some dogs are so friendly, they'll go with anyone who offers them a treat. Or, maybe the thieves used some kind of tranquilliser. My friend the cricket captain said he wondered if his dog might've already been sedated, and gone to his usual sleeping spot under the bush while the thieves were waiting round the corner 'til the coast was clear.'

'We're sitting in this perfect place, having munched our way through half a ton of yummy cake. You wouldn't believe such nasty things could happen round here, would you?'

At once, his face closed. Really closed, as if he'd pulled a shutter across. 'Horrible things happen everywhere. Surely you realise that?'

'Of course I do.' She felt curious about his strong reaction but didn't question him about it. 'And there are people living in Bailsford who have amazing lifestyles. Apart from his shop duties, Granddad's a parish councillor and school governor, so he meets loads of villagers. Most are ordinary, but there's a sprinkling who own fancy cars, hot tubs, swimming pools — you name it.'

'That doesn't mean all those people are happy or well-balanced, Hannah.'

'No, but we're straying from the point here, aren't we?'

'Okay. I'm thinking out loud now. Posh houses. Expensive dogs. Pedigree dogs. You don't have to live in a mansion and be a high earner to own a classy dog. Some people save up for ages to buy the breed they want.'

'You're right about that. Mrs Andrews certainly doesn't give the impression she's loaded, unless she won the Lottery and is keeping it secret,' said Hannah. 'I think what we're both saying is that the dog thief knew exactly where to find what he or she wanted.'

'In other words, they did their homework. One casual visit to my dad's pub would've told them about the vicarage pups. Not so sure how someone would find out about Toffee being left in the utility room sometimes.'

Hannah stared at Ryan. 'Someone up to no good would be on the lookout for clues. A chance remark in the community shop could have led to the thief following Mrs Andrews home. Debbie says she's a huge fan of cinema, and often chats about what she and her husband have seen or are about to see. If Toffee was tied up outside the shop while her mistress was inside — '

'It's all right, Hannah. I get the picture.'

'Should I say something to Mrs Andrews, d'you think? About what might happen to her dog?'

Ryan shrugged. 'It's not my business, but if I were you, I'd just stay positive and hope she does the same. The police may have a handle on this, especially if it's the same gang.'

'You're right. I don't want to frighten her about something that might never happen. I hate to think Ben would be mixed up with such awful people, don't you?'

'Hannah, I don't know what to think. I hardly know him. He might have problems with debt. People who get into trouble because they owe money can easily become desperate enough to grab at something or somebody that promises to help them.'

Hannah was fast realising Ryan displayed a greater knowledge of human nature than she did. But something was bugging her.

'Why come back to your own patch to commit a crime?' She stared solemnly at Ryan. 'Surely that's a stupid thing to do?'

'Not necessarily. If — and it's a big if — Ben really is involved, think how good he'd be at identifying the households who have the expensive dogs. He's lived here all his life, and okay, he's got a job in Bristol, but he often comes home at weekends because I've seen him, although he always ignores me. You saw what he was like when he stopped to talk to you.'

'He definitely uses The Seven Stars.'

'I hardly ever work in the bar, but you'd be surprised what people say when they're drinking and relaxing. They can be very careless sometimes. If I'm right in what I'm thinking, then Master Ben shot himself in the foot when he noticed you and asked his mate to stop in front of your house. The cogs started turning for both of us after that, didn't they?'

'Yes. If he was showing his mate the layout of the village, it'd certainly explain why they were driving down there.' Hannah looked at her watch. 'I think I'll call on Granddad before I go home. I'll pass on that message about Saturday's match and make sure he's got something for his tea.'

'Will you tell him what we suspect?'

She shook her dark hair back from her face. 'Not at the moment. I want to do some research online so I know a bit more about these thieves and what kind of tricks they get up to.'

'I meant to ask you, did Mrs Andrews give you a decent photograph of Toffee?'

'As it happens, she did, but I haven't got around to making new posters yet.'

He fixed her with a very intense stare. 'I'd appreciate it if you could email me her dog's picture.'

'Are you volunteering to make up the posters? I'm going to look on the Internet as soon as I can.'

'Not unless you really don't want to. It's just a little idea I have simmering.'

Hannah took her diary from her bag and pushed it towards him. 'If you write your email address at the back for me, I'll attach the photo.'

'Cheers. As many people as possible should be made aware of the problem so they can take extra care. Not that it'll help poor Mrs Andrews, unless by some miracle Toffee's being held somewhere and somehow gets found.'

'Then we'd better pray for a miracle,' said Hannah.

5

'I'd clean forgotten we were away to Collinswood this weekend,' said Greg.

'No wonder, with a nasty cold like you've had. You should only go to the cricket if you feel up to it.'

'All right, Nurse Ross.' Hannah's granddad pointed to the pile of papers and library books on the table. 'I'm not in the mood for switching on my computer, and I'm tired of crosswords and amateur sleuth stories. Never thought I'd say it but it's true.'

'Do you think amateur detectives are a help or a hindrance?'

'Depends. The fictional ones are usually right. Ones in real life can sometimes get the wrong end of the stick and upset people.'

Hannah, despite telling Ryan otherwise, was tempted to ask her grandfather's advice. 'Can you remember some dog thefts a while back — not in our village but round Collinswood, maybe early last summer?'

Granddad clasped his hands behind his head and thought. 'Can't say it's ringing any bells. Why?'

'I didn't tell you when I called in earlier because I didn't want you to think I was getting too involved.'

'I'm not sure I like the sound of this.'

Hannah told him about Mrs Andrews coming into the shop and how much she missed her dog.

'Poor woman. I don't always get to church on a Sunday, but whenever I do, I always see her and her husband. Quiet people, but when you speak to them, always very pleasant. I get the impression they're creatures of habit.'

'Like they usually go into town on a Wednesday night to visit the cinema.'

'That proves my theory — but how are you involved, love? Apart from offering to do whatever you need to do on social media?'

'I made some posts and alerted the

right people this afternoon before I met Ryan at the Manor for tea.' She smiled. 'What's that look on your face for? You should be pleased I've found someone to hang out with.'

'I can't help how I look! Don't change the subject, please.'

'Okay. So far as we know, the council dog wardens haven't picked up Mrs Andrews' pet. The department told me they'd check, but if she'd already been put into the pound, and she was microchipped, they would've already got in touch with her owner. Mrs Andrews hasn't phoned my mobile, so sadly, I think we can assume Toffee still hasn't come home.'

'So, has the animal been microchipped?'

'Apparently not,' said Hannah. 'It isn't compulsory in England yet, but the time will come.'

Granddad shook his head, a sad expression on his face. 'If the animal really has been made off with and it's not a case of her somehow escaping and running away, you have to wonder if whoever did it left behind any evidence.'

'What, like DNA?'

'Do the police have the time and resources to check for that? But I'm wondering if there were any footprints or tyre tracks. Surely the thief or thieves would have driven here?'

Hannah thought of the tatty vehicle driven by Ben's friend that Ryan had noticed parked near the vicarage. She said nothing. It had rained earlier in the week, and that would have put paid to tell-tale tyre tracks.

'If you have the time and inclination,' her granddad suggested, 'you could ask around the area. See if anyone noticed any dodgy goings-on. These light evenings, people are out and about more. They sit on the patio, mow the lawn, walk to the pub or whatever.'

'Mum said something about village people keeping an eye open for anything suspicious.'

'Ah, that's the Neighbourhood Watch scheme. Well done, Hannah. Though I imagine if anyone involved in that had noticed something, they'd have spoken up by now.'

'It's just occurred to me. The evenings have been lovely and light, but we've had quite a lot of rain since Tuesday morning. A wet murky evening on Wednesday must've kept a lot of people indoors.'

'You're right, love. I switched my heating on, though in summer I try not to do that.'

'You've been poorly. I'm glad you were indoors keeping cosy. But that dismal weather would've been perfect for someone plotting to steal a pet they knew was kept in the utility room. It sounds as if Toffee could only have escaped if someone let her out, and why in the world would anyone want to do that?'

'Hannah, pop the kettle on, would you? I need something to help me think.'

She stood up. 'As a matter of interest, did you know about Mr and Mrs Andrews getting the boy next door to keep an eye on their dog if they were planning to be out for more than a few hours?' Hannah flicked the switch on and took milk from the fridge.

'Hmm? Oh, yes. The youngster sings in the church choir. I don't think it's any secret that he loves helping out. He earns extra pocket money, and he thinks the world of that dog. His mum has a cat and won't hear of getting a puppy, so it's been an ideal situation in some ways.'

'Until now.'

'Indeed. I imagine the poor lad's devastated, but none of this can be his fault, can it?'

'Of course not. He's a child. It wouldn't have crossed his mind that it might be best not to mention how he helps look after Mr and Mrs Andrews' dog sometimes.'

Granddad narrowed his grey eyes. 'You know, Hannah, what bugs me is the thought of someone from the village being involved, although my common sense tells me that must be the case. It's hardly likely that a stranger drove to Bailsford in hopes of sneaking down a driveway and turning a random back-door handle to be greeted by a beautiful pedigree pooch.'

'I agree. Don't you think we have to assume the dog thief targeted that particular house because of a tip-off?'

'You could well be right. By the way, I'm dying of thirst here.'

'It's nearly ready. You should've spoken up earlier.'

'You'll make a good headteacher one day, Hannah.' Granddad rubbed his chin. 'When it comes to speaking up, didn't you say Mrs Andrews told you they'd reported the theft to the police? But the couple probably didn't return home from the cinema until half-ten or so. By the time they'd searched the area and Mr Andrews drove round looking for the dog, it must have been too late to alert people. I believe the

Neighbourhood Watch is a wonderful scheme, but on a weeknight a lot of people are tucked up in bed by ten-thirty. Or the curtains are closed and they're watching TV.'

'What you're saying is, by the time Mrs Andrews made her posters and brought them into the shop, poor little Toffee could've been a hundred miles away.'

'Possibly. What we, as amateur sleuths, have to hope, is that the dog is being safely cared for somewhere and that the thieves strike again, quickly.'

'But that's a horrible thought, Granddad. Surely no one could possibly want that to happen?'

'Of course not. But you have to try and put yourself in the mind of the thief — or, more likely, thieves. If they know people are concentrating on finding this particular dog, events might go one of two ways.'

'Like how?'

'Many people say lightning never strikes twice in the same place. Lots of folk think they're safe in their comfortable routine and can't believe anyone would do anything to upset the applecart.'

'So, should we be alerting everyone in the village? That's not going to be easy.'

'I agree. Not everyone has a computer, and even if they do, they mightn't access the village website.'

'Not everyone uses The Seven Stars, either.'

'Correct. Or the community shop.' Granddad looked a little regretful. 'I'm sorry to say, some folk use this village like a dormitory.'

'People lead busy lives. But do you really think the thieves would come back and steal another dog? Just like that? Wouldn't it be asking for trouble?'

'You tell me, Hannah.'

'They're unlikely to be after animals of mixed ancestry, aren't they?' She placed a mug of tea beside her grandfather.

'Thanks, love. 'Mixed ancestry'? That's

an original description of a mongrel! Maybe '57 Varieties' is old-fashioned nowadays. But you're right, of course. Pedigree puppies and young dogs will fetch a substantial amount of cash when they're sold on. People who just want a dog to love, and maybe got one from a rescue centre, aren't so likely to have their pet stolen.'

'Hang on.' Hannah passed him the biscuit tin. 'I saw a notice somewhere — it must've been in the pub. The vicar's wife is advertising two puppies for sale. Surely you're not saying they could be at risk?'

Granddad dunked a chocolate biscuit in his tea. 'I'm not a gambling man; but let's just say, if I was, I wouldn't bet against it.'

⋆ ⋆ ⋆

Later, when Hannah was jogging round the school playing field, trying to focus her mind upon child psychology rather than dog theft, she didn't notice someone walking in the opposite direction.

'And you don't even have your earbuds in,' said Ryan.

She kept jogging on the spot. 'I was concentrating.'

'Look, I don't want to hold you up. I just wondered if you'd heard anything.'

'About the missing dog, you mean?'

'Yes,' he said patiently.

'Nothing so far, but I have to tell you, Granddad's getting involved.'

'Is that a good thing?'

'I'm not sure. Probably, but I don't want him doing anything too daring.'

Ryan nodded. 'He's in pretty good shape, I guess, but I can't imagine ever getting to be as old as he is.'

Hannah giggled. 'Better not tell him that.'

'Don't worry, I shan't.' He hesitated. 'Dare I ask if he's come up with any suggestions?'

She stopped jigging up and down. 'Do you want to come round later, or are you working tonight?' She couldn't believe she sounded so confident, especially with her heart bumping about like a jumping bean.

'Um, well, I am, actually. I'm working tomorrow night as well. It plays havoc with my social life, but it helps my bank account.'

'Of course,' she said, trying not to show her disappointment.

'How about Saturday afternoon? We could go to the orangery again.'

'Saturday afternoon's good, but why don't you come round to ours? I might even make a cake.' She held her breath.

'Yeah, okay then. Excellent. Will your granddad be there? I mean, um, is this a kind of team-meeting thing?'

'If he goes out at all, he'll be getting on the coach with the cricket team and the rest of their groupies. You should really think about joining them,' she said, giving him a mischievous little glance.

That Sunday-best smile lit up his face. 'Bad girl. Get on with your jogging, and I'll see you around three on Saturday, if we don't bump into one another before.'

She set off again, called 'Bye!' over her shoulder, and wondered what kind of social life he'd meant. Maybe it was the kind of thing people said when they didn't necessarily mean it. But she and Ryan hadn't known one another for long, and why would he share information like that with her? He struck her as a very private person. The Ryan she'd met that Sunday she and Granddad had their lunch in the pub had come over as very professional and competent. She'd been gobsmacked to learn the identity of the talented artist who created those magical watercolours.

Hannah realised she'd become very bored doing circuits around the recreation ground. There was a mixed doubles match taking place on one of the tennis courts, and she found herself wishing she could be out there with them. But if she asked Ryan to give her a game, would he start wondering about her motives? There'd been that muttered comment about girls being manipulative. Life could be so complicated sometimes.

She didn't think she knew any of the four players, but suddenly realised the vicar's wife was among them. Mrs Ferguson could make the ball go pop without a doubt. Probably none of these people was younger than fifty, but they were doing a good job. Hannah paused to watch the vicar's wife serve. Someone yelled out the score. Mrs Ferguson's next serve sent the ball bouncing awkwardly, impossible for the person receiving it to return. The vicar's wife and her partner exchanged high-fives, and Hannah turned away towards the footpath towards the other side of the village and home.

'Hannah?' The person calling sounded surprised. 'I've only just realised it's you. How lovely to see you again.'

Hannah turned around to see the vicar's wife hurrying across the court to the wire netting separating them. 'Oh, hi, Mrs Ferguson. I was just admiring your serve.'

'I don't play often enough, but you know how it is.' She took a swallow of water from a plastic bottle. 'This is hot work. So, are you around for the rest of the summer? You know Jodie's got a coaching job at a summer camp?'

'I think I heard through the grapevine. Yes, that's great. I'm house-sitting for Mum and Dad and my grandfather's roped me in to help at the shop.'

'Yes, so I noticed. It's a brilliant thing to do; two brilliant things, in fact.' She beamed. 'I must tell Jodie I've seen you.'

'Say hi for me.' Hannah decided to ask the question nagging at her. 'So, have you found homes for your puppies yet?'

'My sister wanted two of them, but the others are still with us. We really mustn't keep them, much as I'd like to. My husband's out such a lot, and I'm away all day in term-time, as you know. The mother dog's good as gold on her own, and Susie Evans — our Girl Friday — is a treasure. She does a bit of cooking for us, and most important of all, she doesn't mind walking the dog as well as keeping the place in order.'

'Did you hear the dog belonging to Mr and Mrs Andrews has gone missing?'

The vicar's wife glanced across at her friends. 'I did, yes. I feel so sorry for them. Between you and me, it's no wonder people find it hard to keep their faith with such horrid things going on in the world.'

Hannah nodded, not sure how to react. 'I must let you get back to your game,' she said. 'I'm helping spread the word about that dog being stolen. There's no way she could've got out on her own.'

'I guess not. How about I ask the vicar to give a gentle warning about security this Sunday at all the services? That'll help spread the word.'

'Thanks, Mrs Ferguson. That's very kind.'

'He'll be pleased to help. I'm leaving first thing Monday to spend a few days with my mother in Eastbourne, but I'll make sure Susie remembers not to let any of the dogs into the front garden unless she's out there with them. Not that you'd expect the thief to come back again.'

Hannah watched the woman lope across the court to take her place. Her partner gave Hannah a wave and called out, 'Come on, Fergie, I can't win this match on my own, you know!'

Mrs Ferguson stopped suddenly and turned to face Hannah. 'The place where dogs often get stolen from is the front garden,' she called. 'Thieves don't only operate during the hours of darkness. Just a thought.'

6

Thanks to the ingredients Hannah found in her mother's bottomless store cupboard, topped up by what she bought in the village shop, she assembled everything required for her trial cake bake. She'd checked the Manor House website, but found no recipe for the heavenly cake sampled in the pop-up café. Maybe the proprietors guarded the secret jealously. Fortunately, her mother was a huge fan of *The Great British Bake Off*; and amongst her numerous printouts of recipes, Hannah pounced on one that made her mouth water.

Freed from shop assistant duties over the weekend, Hannah began her preparation early Saturday morning. She was carefully creaming butter and soft brown sugar together in the biggest mixing bowl she could find when she heard the phone in the hall ringing.

Why did her tummy lurch? She wasn't expecting bad news. Most people used her mobile number these days, anyway. As she made her way to the phone, an image of Ryan's face, in smiling mode, floated into her mind's eye. *Get a grip*, she told herself. He'd ring her mobile if he couldn't after all turn up that afternoon. No big deal if that was the case. After all, she hadn't thought of her invitation as being a date.

'Hannah. It's me.'

'Granddad, is everything all right?' She felt relief that it wasn't Ryan ringing to cry off, followed by guilt in case her grandfather had some problem to report.

'Of course it's all right. Why shouldn't it be?'

Hannah brushed flour from the receiver. She'd already weighed out the required amount. Every single ingredient was lined up as if waiting for the Bake Off judges to come along and inspect progress. She was ready to whisk and beat her way to success.

'Just checking,' she said. 'After all, you've been a bit poorly lately.'

'A mere blip, darling. I took a short walk to the duck pond and back, and returned ravenous. So I'm grilling bacon now, if you fancy breakfast.'

She smiled down the phone. 'Aw, thanks Granddad, but I'm having a baking session. If it comes out all right, I'll save you a slice of chocolate cake.'

'Ah, well, that does sound tempting. I rarely eat a cooked breakfast, but I'm off to the cricket in a bit. The coach leaves The Seven Stars at eleven, if you fancy an outing.'

'I'm glad you feel well again, but I, um, have an appointment this afternoon.'

'Let me guess. Mr Wonderful again, is it?'

'Granddad, you're incorrigible. As it happens, Ryan and I are taking the question of the dog thefts very seriously. We're going to discuss how we can help dog owners keep their pets safe. I've already spoken to the vicar's wife.'

That should stop him in his tracks, thought Hannah. She began counting, and reached the number three.

'Crikey. So you've tackled Fergie the Formidable, have you?'

Hannah blinked. 'Sorry?'

'Oh, don't mind me, darling. It's only that our vicar's extremely capable wife has a knack of making me feel like a naughty twelve-year-old again. And that's quite an achievement, considering I'm all of seventy-five!'

Gleefully, Hannah decided Fergie the Formidable's daughter Jodie must take after her mum.

'If you want to pop in later,' he continued, 'I gather we should be home by seven.'

'You have a great day and enjoy yourself, Granddad. Why not go for a drink with the boys when you get back? I'm planning a Saturday night of DVD-watching, so how about we save some cake for Sunday tea?' She held her breath, but he didn't tease her further. Anyway, Ryan was due to help his folks that evening, and from the little she knew of him, she couldn't imagine him letting them down just to keep her company.

Back in the kitchen, she remembered to switch on the oven before picking up her wooden spoon again. She'd left her mum's portable radio on, and suddenly realised she was listening not to pop music but to people talking. Real people. What was more, they were having an animated conversation about dogs. One of them was bemoaning the fact that he hadn't had his pet microchipped before it went missing. Thoughtfully, Hannah whisked eggs while she listened. Someone mentioned the UK Pet Register, and she decided to check that out as a matter of urgency.

She hadn't been aware of the amount of help online when it came to creating a 'missing pet' poster. Mrs Andrews had done her best under difficult circumstances, but Hannah liked the thought of creating another notice with more impact. She hadn't yet got around to researching as she'd told Ryan she intended. Country life was proving to be more demanding than she'd imagined.

The butter and sugar mixture had turned a tempting shade of caramel, its scrumptious smell reminding her of all her childhood birthday cakes combined into one delicious daydream. Carefully, she began adding beaten egg and tablespoons of flour. She blended in cocoa powder, reminding herself to buy a new tin of her father's favourite bedtime drink.

Baking, she decided, was therapeutic; but how those brave amateurs achieved the results they so often did on the television programme, working against the clock and beneath the combined gaze of millions of people, she would never know.

At last, she closed the oven door on

the cake tin, and set her mum's kitchen timer. If she washed up her cooking utensils at once, she could start seeking information from the various organisations available to help dog owners.

* * *

Fresh from the shower — and hoping she really did smell of rain-washed mountain greenery, like the label on the bottle said — Hannah was sitting outside, catching up with her reading, when she heard the front doorbell ring. She glanced at her watch and saw the time was precisely three o'clock. Funny, but she wouldn't have thought of Ryan as a stickler for punctuality.

She walked down the tiled pathway around the side of the house to greet him. He wore baggy black shorts and a dark green T-shirt, and clutched a carrier bag.

He pulled out his earbuds as he saw her. 'Wow, you should always wear that colour. Sea-green really suits you.'

She wasn't accustomed to being with a boy who noticed the way she dressed, but this time she accepted the compliment. 'Thank you. I've been sitting in the garden. It's so lovely again, and I've been cooped up indoors all morning.'

'Me too,' he said, following her.

'Helping in the pub?'

'Working on a project. I'll show you in a bit.'

She turned round to face him. 'That sounds interesting. Oh, I'm pleased to say Granddad felt well enough to go with the cricket team.'

'Cool.'

'I think he was starting to get the fidgets.' Hannah flopped down on one of the patio loungers.

Ryan sat opposite her, perched a little awkwardly. He hugged his carrier bag to his chest.

'Would you prefer to sit at the table?'

'I just wanted your opinion on something. Do you mind?' He got up again and took his carrier bag across to the garden table close to the French doors.

She followed him. 'Of course I don't mind. This sounds intriguing.'

Carefully, he extracted a square package wrapped in tissue paper from the green plastic bag inscribed with the logo *Bailsford Community Post Office and Stores*. Hannah watched him unwrap a framed picture, which he held up for her to inspect.

'Oh, that's definitely Toffee,' she said. 'I should say, the picture looks just like the dog in the photograph. I haven't actually seen her in real life, of course.'

'Nor have I, which is why I wanted to run this past you.'

'Is this for Mr and Mrs Andrews?'

'Yeah. I've used pastel crayons to sketch the animal, and I've done my best to make her portrait lifelike. What d'you reckon?'

'You don't need to explain what you tried to do, Ryan. Anyone can see what a fabulous job you've made. I imagine they'll be thrilled and sad all at the same time. I would be,' said Hannah.

'Maybe I should back off until we know more about . . . well, you know what I'm saying.'

'Until either she's found, or the time comes when it's obvious there's no hope of ever seeing her again?'

'Yeah, that.' He bit his lip.

'Ryan, it's a gorgeous picture. Whatever happens, I think Toffee's owners will be touched to have this souvenir. Have they any idea what you were planning?'

'None at all. I haven't ever spoken to them. The thought came to me when you said you'd been given a decent photo of the little dog.'

'You're a star, Ryan. You really are.'

He looked away hurriedly. Shuffled his feet a bit.

'I'll make tea, shall I?'

'With cake?' He sounded hopeful.

'Of course with cake. Ta-da! Time to show off my work of art.'

'I'd better wrap this picture up again.

111

Maybe I could leave it with you?'

'What for?' She watched his hands, long fingers moving deftly to fold black tissue paper sheets, hiding the image of the golden-bronze dog, drawn on a background the colour of clotted cream. Toffee's beseeching liquid eyes gazed solemnly into the distance, and her expression begged you to pick her up and cuddle her. Stunningly simple. Simply stunning.

Ryan took a step towards her. Hannah, acting on impulse, held out her hand. He reached out for it and came closer still.

'I'd sooner you keep it and give it to them when you think you should. If you really do think my picture's good enough?'

'More than good enough. It's also such a sweet, kind thing to do, Ryan.' *Boys who blush*, thought Hannah, *are the loveliest boys of all.*

'All right, I'll hang on to it for the time being. Now, you can cut two slices of cake while the kettle boils.' She pulled him towards the open French doors.

'Try and stop me! Hey, I like your folks' colour scheme,' he said, glancing round as he followed her inside and his feet met the blond wood floor. 'That rug's fabulous against all the neutral shades. It's like fifty shades of orange.'

She chuckled. 'I got quite a surprise when I returned and saw what they'd been up to. The place looked like one huge jumble sale when I went away.' She suddenly realised she still had hold of his hand. Tried to pull her fingers away, which met with gentle but firm resistance.

'I thought you were looking forward to tea and cake,' she said quietly, looking up at him.

'Not half as much as I was looking forward to seeing you again.' He released his hold on her hand.

'I expect you've missed Jodie being around?'

'Sorry?'

Hannah gulped, instantly regretting her remark. 'Didn't you used to go out with Jodie Ferguson?'

'You've been listening to village gossip.'

She moved towards the door, not daring to drop his father in it. 'Don't tell me you haven't heard comments about me,' she said, smiling at him. 'Taking off with my friends for the best part of a year, leaving Mum and Dad to settle in on their own.'

He shook his head. 'I've only heard good things. It's not your fault your folks decided to up sticks and move to Bailsford at a significant time of your life.'

She caught her breath. He was so supportive. So understanding. She'd been nosey.

Then he pulled the rug from beneath her feet. 'So, what have people been saying about me and Jodie?'

They'd reached the kitchen. Hannah hurried over to fill the kettle, trying to find the right words. Wondering how he'd respond to whatever she had to say.

'All I heard was that you'd hung out together.' She hesitated. 'I wouldn't want anyone to think I was trying to take you away from her.'

'Not an option. I don't belong to Jodie, or to anyone else.'

Hannah turned round to face him. 'I'm so sorry, Ryan,' she gasped. 'I truly didn't mean to upset you.'

She'd only just noticed how his fists were clenched at his sides, when he was across the room and putting his arms around her, not allowing her more than seconds to recognise what was happening. Before she even had time to think how wonderful it felt, being hugged by him.

'If I kissed you, would you chuck me out?' That heartbreaking, brilliant smile had replaced the dark, ominous storm clouds.

Hannah looked up at him. Sometimes she moaned to her mum that she wasn't tall enough to look elegant. Now she felt she was just the right height for six-foot Ryan, snuggled against his chest so he nuzzled his chin on her head.

Her voice came out muffled. Not mature and casual. In no way indicating how often her day included young, attractive men requesting a kiss.

'What if I said yes?'

He hugged her even tighter. 'I'd walk away, but I wouldn't stop being your friend, Hannah. If that's what you'd like of course.'

She tilted her head back so there was space between them and she could meet his steady, blue-eyed gaze.

'My English teacher at school used to remind us to show, not tell. Does that answer your question?'

She heard him catch his breath. He bent his head. Hannah closed her eyes and let the carousel whirl her round and round until she was breathless and laughing in his arms and wishing the moment would go on and on forever.

'Your cake is lush, Hannah. I think it's even nicer than the one we had at the orangery.'

'Really? I suppose it's not too bad.' She didn't want to show him how proud she was. 'I was totally paranoid about getting the proportions right.'

'Yeah? You should apply for that Bake Off thing my mother goes on about.'

'My mum watches that programme too. But I'd never get selected. I'd be sure to make a mess of the preliminaries, or whatever they call them.'

'You might surprise yourself. From what you've told me, you're good at exams. And you must've done well at your interview to get accepted for your training course.'

'That's different. I'm not confident enough to put myself up in front of people.'

'Yet you want to be a teacher? Weird.'

'Nothing weird about wanting to teach, Ryan!'

He smiled back at her. 'You know what I mean.'

'I'd rather be in charge of a classroom full of five-year-olds than face those scary judges.'

He glanced at his watch. 'Do you fancy a walk? I haven't had much exercise today, and I'm working this evening. Sadly.'

'I thought you were glad of the money.'

'Sure. But I'd rather hang out with you.'

She thought how lovely it would be to spend the rest of the day with him. Make a big omelette with oven chips and a salad later. Maybe share a bottle of her dad's wine and talk about everything under the sun. Compare notes about their travels. Watch a DVD, snuggled up side-by-side on the sofa.

He was gazing at her.

'Sorry! Yes, a walk would be good.'

'Are you sure you're okay, staying here without your folks? Sure you don't want to move in with Greg?'

She shook her head so her dark hair shimmied and settled around her face again. 'I love Granddad to bits, but he'd drive me bonkers. He likes his routines, and I'd drive him bonkers too!'

Ryan reached for her hand. 'Well, if you ever feel the need for a bodyguard, just let me know.'

She felt herself blushing. Just when she thought she was in complete control, this young man had the knack of dismantling her determination to keep their relationship on a friendly basis only.

He was looking troubled. 'You can trust me, Hannah. I'm not some slimeball trying to take advantage of you.'

She shook her head. 'I know that, silly. It's just that I didn't think staying friends with you — as in, friends and no more — would be so difficult.'

The rainbow smile appeared again.

'Come on, funny-face, let's go walkies.'

'Give me two ticks.'

'I'll wait outside,' he said.

She ran upstairs to collect a cobwebby pink cardigan and kick off her sandals to push her feet into soft leather loafers. Not that there should be any puddles still lying around. When she got downstairs again, she checked the front door was properly secured, and went out through the back, locking it behind her.

Ryan was standing in the driveway, looking around at the other houses.

'Have you got to know any of your neighbours yet?' He took hold of her hand and they fell in step, walking to the gate.

'Like my dad says, only as far as passing the time of day. One side, there's a couple that commute to Gloucester. I've hardly seen them at all. The other side, there's a family with two teenage children. They seem nice, but the boy's probably going through the caveman phase, so he keeps his head down if he sees me and only grunts if he really has to.'

'Ha,' said Ryan. 'To think I used to be like that.'

'Used to be?' She joked.

He squeezed her hand. 'Any dogs in this close?'

'Probably. I haven't noticed any in the gardens, but I've seen the odd one go by on the end of a lead. Maybe I should be more observant after the Toffee incident.'

Ryan stopped walking suddenly.

'What's wrong?'

'I could be mistaken but I think I just saw that guy with the ponytail again.'

'Ben's mate? Where?'

'Disappearing down a driveway. It's that house with the massive hydrangea bushes.'

'I wasn't looking that way.'

'I could be mistaken. He won't be the only man who wears his hair in a ponytail.'

'I can't think of anyone living round here who'd fit that description, but I still don't know too many people.'

'Do you mind if we walk back to your

place as if we've forgotten something?' He spoke out of the corner of his mouth.

She felt laughter bubble up, but did her best to contain it. 'Okay, Mr Bond. Make like we're in a spy movie.'

'When you're back inside, could you jot down the registration of that dirty white van parked outside the house with the brass lamps either side of the front door?'

'You really are taking this seriously, aren't you?'

'Oh, yes. I've had a funny feeling about Ben and his mate, and I'd just like to make sure Mr Ponytail is some sort of tradesman and not someone about to commit dog theft.'

They walked on in silence. A few yards from Hannah's house, she let go of his hand and strode ahead. 'Shan't be long,' she called. 'I hate not having my phone with me.'

She hurried round the back of the house, let herself into the kitchen, and pulled her mother's memo pad towards her. The pencil had rolled on to the floor, but she repeated the registration number of the scruffy van until she'd written it down.

Outside, Ryan hadn't moved from the spot, but was playing with his phone. He looked up as she approached. 'All right?'

'Yep.'

She snuck her hand into his and he looked down at her.

'What?'

'Nothing,' he said. 'I suppose there's no way of us getting round the back of that house where the van's parked?'

'No chance. These properties are all 'custom-built to maximise privacy and security'. That's a quote from the sales particulars.'

'Fair enough. I wonder if the guy will be long, doing whatever it is he's doing.'

'We're going to look a bit silly, hanging around here. Shall we walk down to the end? If the van driver leaves, he has to go back the way he came. There's only one way in and out of the close.'

'Excellent,' said Ryan. 'What if we stand under the bus shelter? Look as if we're checking the timings. No one could think anything odd about that.'

'It's not a bad idea anyway. Dad's left the car in an airport car park, so if I want to go to town, I'll have to use the bus. I haven't needed to check yet, but I bet there's only one or two coming through here every day.'

'It must seem weird to you, having lived all that time in London.'

She shrugged. 'Travelling with the girls acted like a kind of bridge between my past and my future. Even if I have withdrawal symptoms leaving all those fabulous shops behind, so far I haven't felt marooned living in Bailsford.' She didn't add, *thanks to meeting you*.

At the top of the close they crossed the road over to the bus stop. Ryan put his arm round her shoulders as they peered at the timetable.

'Wow. Looks like there's one designed

for people going into town to work or shop. And that's it until lunchtime.'

'Hannah, I get to use my mother's car if she doesn't need it, so I can always drive you, as long as you give me a bit of notice.'

'Thanks, but I wouldn't want to use you as a taxi service.'

'Don't look now,' he said. 'I spy one dirty white van heading down Manor View towards us.'

'D'you really mean I shouldn't look?'

'Just pretend not to look, but try to see if you recognise the driver.'

'I'll go on chattering about rubbish things, shall I?'

'No change there, then.'

She mock-punched him. He doubled up, pretending to stagger so he ended up further along the pavement. One swift glance at the van driver, now waiting to turn left out of the quiet road, showed her that his attention was focused upon Ryan. And he was definitely Ben's ponytailed friend.

Hannah waited until the van turned

left again at the junction. 'That was clever. I don't think he saw me looking at him, he was so busy looking at you reeling about.'

'Thanks. He must've recognised us, but he mightn't think we remembered him. If he's up to no good, he won't want to meet anyone's eyes. All the time Ben was chatting to you, Mr Ponytail kept his head down, and I wouldn't mind betting he was very cheesed off about Ben insisting on trying to chat you up.'

'But if he didn't want to show his face, why would he have gone into the pub with Ben?'

'Good point.' Ryan thought for a moment. 'Maybe I've got it wrong. Maybe he does want to be seen around the village. That way, if he's a familiar face, he won't seem a threat.'

7

After Hannah said goodbye to Ryan on the village green, she did as he asked and visited the house where the young man in the van had called. She pressed the front doorbell, and surprisingly quickly, an elderly woman wearing a caftan swirling with rainbow shades answered her ring.

'You must be Hannah?'

'Goodness, yes, that's me. Sorry, but I don't know your name.'

'Deirdre Warner.' The woman held out her hand. 'Your parents said you'd be living in the house while they were off cruising. Is this a social call, dear, or did you need something?'

'I don't want to interrupt your Saturday evening.'

'You won't. I've been having pictures and framed photos hung. The bloke's made a very good job of it, too. Come and take a look while you tell me what I can do for you.'

The woman stepped back, allowing Hannah to enter the hallway. 'These are all my own work,' she said.

'Fantastic.'

Hannah waited while Mrs Warner explained where each of her views had been taken before following her into a sitting room that, with so much pink in the decor, appeared bathed in a rosy glow. But the effect worked, kind of, decided Hannah. And she spotted a watercolour she suspected must have been painted by Ryan.

'Is that a painting by Ryan from The Seven Stars?'

'It is. I adore Ryan Hawkins' work. He's set for a successful career, in my humble opinion.'

Hannah nodded. 'He's so good at creating fantastic worlds with loads to look at.'

'I like art that I can go on enjoying, finding something different each time I look at it. What about the rest of the paintings?'

'You have some great pictures.' She turned to face Mrs Warner. 'So, does this tradesman you mentioned live locally? My dad's trying to make a list of plumbers and carpenters, etcetera — people who do a good job.'

'This young man's very tidy and he gets on with it. He's not exactly chatty, like some of them are. I wouldn't dare try banging nails in my walls, so I asked round the neighbours and one said someone knocked at her door last week, asking if she had any jobs needing doing.'

'Did she employ him?'

'Yes. He fixed a wonky curtain rail and screwed a door-handle back on her kitchen unit.'

'So, he's a local person?'

'No idea. All I have is a mobile phone number.'

'Didn't he leave his card, in case you wanted anything else doing?'

'No. I asked for one, but he said he

was planning to have flyers printed once he was sure he can get enough work.'

'Fair enough,' said Hannah, mind working furiously. 'What was his name again?'

'Ah, now didn't that give me a chuckle! The young fellow's called Jack Russell. As in, the dog.'

* * *

Hannah relayed the whole of this conversation to Ryan next morning on the village green, where she bumped into him while on her way to The Seven Stars. They sat on a bench near the duck pond, watching mallards sail serenely over the water's surface, now and then each duck dipping its beak in hopes of a tasty titbit.

'You can't take that name seriously, surely?' Hannah asked.

'It does seem unlikely he's really called Jack Russell.'

'Sense of humour?'

'Maybe.'

'If it's made up, it's a bit silly, considering most people would easily remember it.'

'Did you look it up online?' Ryan asked.

'Of course, but as you'd expect, no handyman business of that name turned up in my search. All that information about dogs made my eyes glaze over. I also learnt about the England cricketer as well as a company that makes clothing.'

'So what's our next step?'

'You're asking me?'

'Yep.'

Hannah sighed. 'I'll print off new posters later, after I've called on Granddad. We can't very well stick up a notice in the shop saying *WARNING — Have You Seen This Man?*, now, can we?'

'Probably not advisable. Have you posted something on the Bailsford website yet?'

'Oh, yes. I tried not to make it sound

too alarming. But I suggested it probably wasn't a good idea to leave a dog out in the front garden in case anybody was roaming about, looking to pick up the right kind of breed.'

'Good for you. There can't be too many pedigree dogs in this village, but to lose any dog's bad enough, without any more going missing.'

'I didn't want to make Mrs Andrews feel bad about leaving Toffee behind an unlocked door, so I mentioned security in general.'

Ryan nodded. 'That had to be a planned operation. We know that. I wonder if the police have other cases on their books that might point to a gang being at work.'

'I haven't a clue. Maybe they'll release a statement if they have.' Hannah checked her watch. 'I'd better go and be a dutiful granddaughter.'

'When will I see you?' Ryan rose from the bench too.

'Do you mean as part of our super-efficient amateur detective team;

or, um, socially?'

He reached out to smooth a tendril of dark hair behind her ear. 'Whatever. As long as I get to spend some time with you soon.'

A little jolt inside her proved he had the power to make a sunny day seem even sunnier. For moments, she forgot what she'd planned to say, and swallowed hard. 'Granddad's taken out a chicken casserole Mum left in his freezer, so we won't be eating at the pub today.'

He nodded. 'We've got a lot of bookings, so it'd be difficult to spend much time with you anyway.'

She made up her mind. 'Would you like to come and watch a DVD with me later, if you're not working?'

Rainbow smile moment! 'There's definitely no restaurant food on a Sunday night. What time shall I arrive?'

'Any time after six.'

'Cool. I think I'll take a few duck photographs before I go inside. There are some fantastic shadows on the water, too. I really can't ignore those.'

When she looked back over her shoulder, Ryan appeared focused on capturing what she knew he observed in a totally different way from the chocolate-box scene most people saw. She wondered what his vivid imagination saw lurking or cavorting beneath the surface. Maybe, if she got lucky, he'd share his ideas with her.

★　★　★

'In here, Hannah.'

To her relief, she heard her grandfather call her from the sitting room as she let herself in the back way and closed the door behind her.

'Hope you didn't mind my using Mum's key, but I couldn't make you hear.' She walked in to find Greg sitting in front of his laptop.

'Did you knock? I didn't hear you.'

'Of course I did. I wondered if you were hungover after yesterday!' She didn't dare reveal her moment of panic

134

when he hadn't answered her knock.

'Tut-tut. I haven't been hungover since I was eighteen and drank too many pints of beer. I vowed then never to put myself through that dreadful experience again. Ever.'

'Good for you.' She patted his hand and knelt beside him. 'I'm being nosey, but I'm interested to see what's caught your attention.'

'I'm looking at some of the newspaper websites, checking if there's anything about missing dogs.'

'That's a good idea. Any luck?'

'Nothing recent. I did wonder if the person who took Toffee came from miles away, rather than somewhere close to Bailsford. But in that case, it'd still be a local theft, even if the thief and the dog ended up many miles from here.'

Hannah nodded patiently. Her granddad was thinking aloud. Sometimes he told her things she'd heard many times before. But his mind remained sharp and enquiring. He could remember historical events and dates she hadn't a clue about. No way would she interfere with his train of thought. Sure enough, she didn't have long to wait.

'Ah!'

Hannah got to her feet. 'That casserole smells wonderful. Do you need me to do anything in the kitchen?'

'It's all sorted, darling. Just let the old cogs and wheels turn a bit longer. You can pour us a glass of cider each, if you like.'

When she came back with their drinks, he was scribbling on a notepad, but looked up as she sat opposite.

'What are the conditions a thief needs?' He tapped his front teeth with his pencil.

'Um, hours of darkness are probably good. Houses left unattended? Bad weather must be helpful — so there aren't many dog walkers and joggers around. Insider knowledge. Ability to disable a burglar alarm.'

'Well done, darling. In certain cases,

I'd add desperation.'

'Isn't that more relevant to long ago, like the convicts who were given the choice of being hanged or being shipped off to Australia?'

'Punishments were incredibly harsh centuries back, considering some of the crimes were things like a parent stealing a loaf of bread to stop their children from starving. Nowadays people can be tempted into crime because they've run up huge debts. Or sometimes they see an opportunity to make a few hundred pounds without too much hassle, and the temptation's too great to resist.'

Hannah took a sip of cider. 'So Toffee's thief used more than one of the conditions we've thought up?'

Granddad nodded. 'In this particular case, I'd plump for insider knowledge being the big factor. Everything points to someone knowing the Andrews' house would be unoccupied that Wednesday evening. They also probably knew this would be an easy pinch. Most dogs, even if they bark at first, like being given food, and it sounds as if Toffee was gentle by nature.'

'And friendly,' added Hannah.

'She was probably whisked away before darkness set in. She's not a very big animal, and whoever took her probably came armed with some kind of basket or pet carrier. Or used a big cardboard box, even a rug, to transport her between the utility room and the vehicle.'

'Using a vehicle familiar to people because it's been seen so often in the village!'

'Perhaps, but not necessarily.'

'I'd better tell you about my visit to Mrs Warner.'

'Another formidable female.'

Hannah shook her head. 'You might say that, but I found her quite easy to talk to. She was singing the praises of a handyman who'd recently hung the pictures and photographs she'd been looking forward to putting on display.'

'Did you get his number?'

'That's the interesting bit. All she had was Jack Russell's mobile number. And we all know how easy it is to buy a cheap phone and then throw it away when it's no longer needed.'

'Jack Russell? Really?'

'I thought you'd appreciate the name. The thing is, have we the right to ask people whether they've used someone called Jack Russell for household work, odd jobs and the like?'

Granddad nodded his head so vigorously, his dandelion clock mane of white hair rippled as if blown by the wind. 'Indeed we do. From what I've heard about young Ryan's and your conclusions, I think it's important we find out more about this individual.'

'We can start tomorrow at the shop, and if I text Ryan, he might be able to ask some of his dad's regulars.'

Her grandfather looked thoughtful. 'Not sure about that. Why would young Ryan be interested in home maintenance?'

'Whoops. You're right. It'd be much

more appropriate if Mr Hawkins did the asking.'

'That would be helpful. We can hardly go round knocking on doors, especially on a Sunday.'

'But we do need to eliminate Jack Russell from our investigations,' said Hannah.

'I doubt that'll be easy, but if we happen to find someone who noticed that vehicle parked outside the Andrews' property last Wednesday evening, I reckon that'd be something the police might be very interested in knowing.'

8

On Monday morning at the shop, Hannah looked up from replenishing the chocolate selection as the doorbell pinged.

'Oh, good! Hannah, I wonder if you could do me a massive favour.' The vicar's wife, dressed in practical denim skirt and jacket, stood clutching her handbag to her chest.

'I'll try. You look as if you're in a hurry, Mrs Ferguson.'

'I'm off to visit my mother for a few days but we're out of rice milk at home and there's none in the freezer.'

'I'll just check we have some. I know it's only your husband and two other people we order it for. Hang on — ' Hannah checked the refrigerated section. 'There's one carton left. Did you want to take it?'

Mrs Ferguson looked — amazingly,

in Hannah's opinion — slightly embarrassed. 'I wonder — could you possibly be an angel and drop it into the vicarage after your shift, Hannah?'

'I guess. It's hardly out of my way. Will the vicar be at home?'

'No. My husband's away all day at a conference, but Susie's due in this morning, and she's agreed to stay until he gets back. I didn't want to leave the house unattended — not with the puppies there, you understand.'

'Don't worry. I'll drop this round for you. Anything else you might have forgotten?'

'If I have, I'm sure my husband will manage without whatever it is until tomorrow. But the rice milk's a bit specialist, so I'm glad I popped in.' She rummaged for her purse. 'You're a star, Hannah. Thank you so much.'

Hannah rang up the purchase.

'Put the change in the box for the church roof fund, please!' Mrs Ferguson opened the door and closed it with a bang, cutting in half Hannah's 'Have a good trip!'.

The air seemed charged with turbulence, she thought, smiling to herself. At least Fergie the Formidable had remembered in time to save her poor husband from being deprived of his breakfast cereal.

Throughout the rest of the morning, Hannah made sure shoppers checked out her updated poster. She asked several people about the handyman known as Jack Russell. One person, who introduced herself as mum to the lad who'd been keeping Toffee company and seeing to her needs while her master and mistress were out, proved very helpful.

'Mr and Mrs Andrews don't go out in the evenings except for their Wednesday cinema visits,' she said. 'It's when they have a day out to go brass-rubbing, or whatever it is, that they ask my son to call in on Toffee. They're devoted to that animal, and so is he. Cried himself to sleep he did, after he heard the news.'

'I'm sure she's being looked after properly,' said Hannah soothingly. 'She may still turn up.'

'Let's hope so,' said the woman. 'Mr and Mrs Andrews have no children of their own, and they're grieving, poor souls.'

'I can imagine.' Hannah paused while her customer selected apples, plus a cauliflower that looked as if it could easily take a prize at the forthcoming flower and produce show.

'I hope you don't mind my asking, but have you ever noticed an old white van parked in the village? It's not sign-written, but the driver seems to be offering to do odd jobs. I think he's only been coming to Bailsford over the last couple of weeks.'

The woman placed a pack of Cheddar cheese in her wire basket and approached the till with her purchases.

'I know the one you mean. The young man knocked at the door one day last week. I had my hands in the washing-up bowl, and by the time I got to the front, he was wandering down the path at the side of our house. He heard me call to him and came back, full of apologies. Said he'd wondered if I was out the back, hanging washing or whatever.'

'Can you remember what he looked like?'

'Well, he had a ponytail, so that's the main thing I remember. I hate that 'man bun' expression.' She wrinkled her nose. 'He had a pale face — stubbly chin like lots of them nowadays and I suppose you'd say he was taller than average. I'm not too great at accents, but I remember he was quite well-spoken.'

'Okay. You know how it is when you move to a different area. My father's building up a list of trustworthy tradesmen. Did the young man do any odd jobs for you?'

'He was out of luck. I told him my husband's a whiz at DIY.'

'I see. From what people have said,

this Jack Russell seems interested in whether people have pets.'

'He certainly asked me whether we had a dog. I told him no way, as we already had one very spoilt moggy. Maybe he's allergic to animal fur? More likely, he wanted to know whether some hulking great canine might appear from nowhere and knock his ladder flying!'

★　★　★

Susie Evans enjoyed working for Bailsford's vicar and his wife. Apart from needing the money, she took pride in cleaning the spacious vicarage. Especially when the two Ferguson children were living away from home. Not that they were kids any more. She'd known them when they were little dots going to the village primary school while her own two attended high school in the nearest town. Nowadays the primary school children were bussed to a larger village to be educated.

Susie arrived at ten o'clock as usual.

Except that today, she was booked to stay until the vicar returned in the early evening. In the kitchen, she said hello to the mother dog and her two remaining pups, closed the door behind her, and gathered her cleaning equipment from the cupboard beneath the stairs. After she'd carried the vacuum cleaner upstairs, she came back down and collected dusters, polishes and cleaning sprays.

Mrs Ferguson's side of the big front bedroom looked as though burglars had ransacked it; but such a muddle wasn't unusual, certainly not in term-time when Mrs F frequently ran late, as she explained it. Time and time again she talked of telephone callers keeping her, hoping to find the vicar on the other end of the line but happy to speak to his other half.

Mrs F taught French at the high school in the nearest town, and Susie reckoned she must be superhuman, with all the plates she needed to keep in the air. It was no hardship to pick up discarded clothing and hang it in the wardrobe. As for the vicar — Susie couldn't hold back a smile when she thought of the vicar — he was the exact opposite of his wife. On the cabinet his side of the bed stood a modest pile of books, one of which was always the Holy Bible. The others were assorted books borrowed from the mobile library van — some of which, Susie privately felt, were a little bloodthirsty for a clergyman.

She had hours ahead of her, but plenty of chores aside from her usual housekeeping duties. Susie had promised to put a casserole together so Mr F had enough for the next few nights, while his wife visited her elderly mum. There were strawberries and raspberries to pick. Susie had instructions to take some home for her family, and also to drop some off to the octogenarian couple living at the end of Susie's lane. She'd be freezing some too, of course.

Last but not least came the doggy family. Susie could never remember which breed they belonged to. Whatever it was, the dog that fathered the latest litter had been carefully selected, and Sasha had produced four beautiful puppies. Two had already gone to Mrs Ferguson's sister, and the remaining two would be sold to the right person or persons. Susie had her instructions. Should anyone ring and enquire, she was to take their phone number so the vicar could call back and arrange an appointment to meet the puppies.

Everything was clear in Susie's mind. The washing machine was rumbling through its cycle, so maybe she'd go downstairs and make herself a coffee. By the time she'd drunk it, she could hang the washing in the back garden.

Perfect timing. Susie was rinsing her mug when she heard the machine judder to the end of its spin. This seemed a good opportunity to let the dogs out while she kept an eye on them. That particular instruction was under-lined in red pen on Mrs F's list: *Do not on any account leave Sasha and the pups alone on the front lawn.* Well, Susie wouldn't even risk leaving them alone in the back garden. In her mind's eye, she'd formed a clear picture of the kind of ruffian who'd steal a dog in hopes of making easy money. Words like *shifty, ruthless* and *menacing* accompanied the unsavoury image, fuelled by the Bill Sykes character in *Oliver!*, the musical Susie had once seen in London.

She went outside to check the side gate was closed so the dogs couldn't wander into the front garden. She let them out and, humming her favourite hymn, pegged washing on the line. Sasha, the mother dog, was sniffing around the vegetable patch while her two remaining pups frolicked on the grass.

It was at this point that Susie heard the front doorbell ring. Lowering her hands after hanging the last garment, she gave a quick glance at the dogs and hurried back inside.

'Good morning.' Susie had scarcely

opened the front door before she heard the greeting. A smartly-dressed woman standing on the paved area outside took off her sunglasses and gave Susie a big smile. 'Mrs Ferguson? I wonder if it's convenient for me to have a look at the puppies you're selling?'

'I'm afraid Mrs Ferguson's not here just now.'

'Oh, dear.' The woman bit her lip. 'I realise I should have rung ahead, but I only just heard from a friend that this particular breed of puppy was being advertised for sale, and I couldn't resist driving over. I've always longed to own a Lhasa Apso, and at this stage of my life, it seems the time is right.'

Susie considered. This woman had a strangely high voice. She felt as if she recalled it from somewhere, but didn't like to ask. Maybe she was thinking of a character in a soap, or someone she'd heard on the radio. The main thing was, the visitor knew exactly what breed the puppies were. Susie always recognised the name when she heard it, but couldn't for the life of her remember it, let alone spell it. It surely wouldn't hurt to let the lady see the puppies? But she had her instructions.

'What name is it, please? I'll need to take your details, so the vicar can ring you tonight and arrange a time for you to come back if that's what you decide to do.'

The woman sighed. 'It's a shame, but rules are rules, I guess. My name's Sheila McCarthy. That's Mrs. I can give you my address and phone number if you let me have pen and paper.'

'All right, Mrs McCarthy. I'll show you into the study. Mr Ferguson always uses it when his parishioners call,' said Susie.

'You're very kind. I can't believe I was silly enough to drive all this way, only to be disappointed.' Her face crumpled and she opened her handbag and took out a pale pink handkerchief.

Susie felt a pang. 'Well, I can't see any harm in bringing one puppy through at a time, so you can have a quick look.'

'Oh, would you really? I wouldn't want you to get into trouble on my account.'

'I'm sure the vicar will be sympathetic when I explain to him. And I don't think the mother dog will get annoyed. She's used to me being around. I helped Mrs Ferguson when Sasha was giving birth to her pups.'

'How wonderful for you.' The woman smiled. 'I imagine they're old enough to leave their mum now?'

'Oh, yes. The first two have already gone to a good home.'

'Well, if I fall in love with one of the others, he or she will be treasured, that's for sure. Oh, I left my car parked outside the vicarage wall so as not to block the driveway. I hope that's okay.'

'That's fine. I'll be back in a mo.' Susie scuttled off to find the dogs had wandered back inside. Sasha lay in her basket, and the two puppies frisked towards Susie when she entered the room. She picked up one and kissed its forehead. 'Come on, Juliet,' she said. 'A nice lady wants to talk to you.'

Juliet's brother Jupiter whined as if disappointed. 'Back in a bit, sweetie,' said Susie, setting off with the puppy in her arms and using one foot to push the door shut behind her.

The visitor rose when Susie arrived. 'Oh, my goodness,' she said. 'These dogs are so adorable. Aren't they just like teddy bears? Already I love this one to bits. Girl or boy?'

'This is Juliet. I'll put her down for you.'

Carefully, Susie lowered the little dog to the carpet, a carpet upon which hundreds of pairs of feet had stood and walked. Susie always found herself thinking of the starry-eyed couples turning up to discuss their weddings; proud parents wanting babies baptised; and, more poignantly, bereaved parishioners needing help over the delicate matter of saying goodbye to their loved ones.

This morning was potentially a happy occasion. Mrs McCarthy dropped to her knees and held out a hand towards Juliet to let the puppy sniff at her inquisitively.

Susie looked around, decided it was somewhat stuffy inside the little room, and walked across to open the window. A gentle breeze wafted inside, riffling the threadbare curtains. Obtaining a new pair sat high on the things-to-do list, according to her employer.

Susie stood watching the woman petting the puppy until she heard the phone in the sitting room begin to ring.

'Oh dear, do you mind if I shut you in with Juliet while I answer that? It'll be someone for the vicar.'

'Of course. You go ahead,' said Mrs McCarthy. 'I'm quite happy making a fuss of this little one while you're gone.'

Susie closed the door carefully behind her and hurried towards the phone, wishing it was like the old days when there was one old-fashioned handset on the hall table. Several years ago, the vicarage telephone system had been changed; so while there was one unit in the sitting room, the second phone meandered around the house as and when required, until it needed recharging and had to be swapped with the sitting room one.

She picked up the receiver and heard the telephone caller respond. He sounded a little bored to Susie's ears. Sounded as though he'd repeated his sales pitch a thousand times before. She thought at first this was a cold call, and waited to stop the flow and give him a polite thanks but no thanks.

Until the caller said, 'So, will you tell the vicar John Franks rang about the quotation he requested?'

'Is this a church matter or something personal?'

'All I can say is it's to do with the proposed kitchen renovation. Bit of both, seeing it's a vicarage, d'you think?'

Susie hesitated. She'd assumed money must be scarce if even new curtains were classed as a luxury. 'I know nothing about any renovation. Maybe it's best if you ring back this evening when the vicar's at home.'

'Mr Ferguson said to leave a message with his housekeeper if he wasn't around. I take it you're the lady in question?'

'Well, yes, I suppose so.'

'Good. He'll want to know his options, so do you have a pen and paper handy?'

Susie reached for the notepad. 'Go ahead,' she said, and promptly dropped the pen. 'Oh, sorry — hang on a mo.' She had to get her specs out of her apron pocket.

John Franks remained on the line. He began to speak rapidly and quite quietly.

'Sorry, could you repeat that?' Susie strained to hear. She hated having to grasp technical details. This barrage of measurements meant nothing to her. The salesman droned on about a special discount for a swift agreement to begin work before the month's end.

Susie, always polite to other people, had wondered at first if this was a nuisance call to swat away like a troublesome winged insect. But, on hearing Mr Franks had important information for the vicar, this obviously couldn't happen. When she'd written down the message — including an eye-watering sum of money — to relay to the vicar, Susie said goodbye and, with a feeling of relief, put down the phone.

* * *

Hannah, having designed an eye-catching flyer warning dog owners to be extra-cautious about where they left their pets, was pausing here and there to push leaflets through letterboxes.

She was outside the gates of the vicarage, about to go and knock on the door to give the housekeeper the forgotten item, when she saw the woman — who she imagined must be the Girl Friday Mrs Ferguson had mentioned

— rush through the front door and come running down the drive. Hannah remembered her name, and called to her.

'Susie? Is something wrong?'

The woman pulled up. Stared at Hannah. Pushed her hands through her hair and wailed, 'Oh, dear! Something terrible has just happened, and I'm at my wits' end.'

'This can't be to do with the vicar's pressing need of rice milk for his morning porridge?'

'What? No! This is about a missing puppy.' Susie's lower lip trembled. 'Did you notice a woman carrying a puppy come out just now?'

'Oh, please don't say we have another case of dog theft in the village!'

'Yes! No! Oh dear, I don't know. She seemed such a nice lady. Dressed very prettily.' Susie gulped. 'She said she wanted to buy one of the puppies. How could someone like her be a dog thief?'

'So this person came in response to Mrs Ferguson's advertisement?'

'Yes. But she's vanished, taking one

of the puppies with her.'

'Let's check outside, then. See if she's taken it to show someone. She must have come by car.' Hannah hurried out of the gateway and checked up and down the road, with no success. Susie was still standing in the same position as Hannah walked back.

'There's no sign of a woman or any vehicle parked in the road.'

'Oh, dear, let's go inside. I didn't mean to be rude and I don't think we can do anything useful by hanging around out here. I imagine the baddies are well on their way to wherever it is they're taking little Juliet.'

'You must be devastated.'

'I really think I've been duped. Conned. Made an absolute fool of by someone I took totally at face value, and now what am I going to tell the vicar when he comes back later?' Susie burst into tears. 'I'll lose my job for sure.' Sobs wrecked her small frame.

'Oh, poor you.' Hannah hugged the older woman round the shoulders and guided her through the open front door. 'You need a hot drink. You're in shock. Of course the vicar and his wife won't sack you. From what Mrs Ferguson told me, they obviously think the world of you.'

'I deserve to lose my job for being so stupidly trusting! And I mustn't waste time drinking tea while that dear little puppy's out there somewhere.'

Hannah spread her hands, feeling useless. 'I don't have a car. Do you know what sort of vehicle this woman was driving?'

'No idea. She said she'd parked outside the vicarage, not wanting to block the driveway. I thought that was very considerate of her. I let her in, took her into the study, and went to fetch little Juliet. I remembered to close the kitchen door into the hallway behind me so the other dogs couldn't wander. After that, everything happened so quickly.'

Hannah had a sudden, awful thought. 'So you're absolutely sure

Sasha and the other puppy are safely inside?'

Susie's face contorted. 'Yes. Oh, I do hope so. Maybe I'd better check and make sure.' She ran across the hallway, Hannah in close pursuit, and opened the kitchen door very cautiously. 'Thank goodness. Yes, Sasha and Jupiter are safe and sound.'

'Sit down, Susie. I'll put the kettle on. I'm used to a kitchen range like this. Mum and Dad had one installed, though it's not on at the moment. We've got a small electric cooker as well.' Hannah knew she was gabbling nonsense, but wanted to try and calm Susie down.

Her gaze switched to the mother dog and her remaining puppy curled up beside the big pine dresser. Two pairs of brown eyes were watching her every move. They were so gorgeous.

Susie sank on to a chair. 'I let the woman — she said her name was Sheila McCarthy — I let her wait in the study while I fetched the girl puppy to show her. She seemed so desperate to see them, and I took pity on her, coming all that way.'

'What happened then?' Hannah's fingers itched to ring the police, but she knew Susie needed to go through how she'd acted. Tears were probably still close.

'I heard the phone ringing. I asked the woman if she'd mind if I answered it. Part of my job is to take messages for the vicar.' She hesitated. 'I'd opened the window as it seemed stuffy in the study.'

'This is the ground floor we're talking about?'

'It is. I can see now that while I was answering the phone, the woman must have climbed through the window and carried Juliet down the drive.'

Hannah looked around. 'Seems to me it's a little too convenient, that phone call coming just after you'd let this Sheila McCarthy into the house. I get the feeling this is a put-up job. She must've had an accomplice who rang the vicarage and kept you talking while she made her getaway.'

'But how would these people know the layout of the house? How would they know the Fergusons weren't at home?'

Hannah grimaced. 'I suspect this is a very efficient gang. The puppy's been taken in different circumstances from poor Toffee, but it's blindingly obvious that a lot of homework's gone into this scam.'

'You seem to know a lot about it.'

'I've been helping Mrs Andrews — the lady whose dog was stolen last week. There's so much we can do via social media these days; but so far, sadly, there have been no sightings of her pet.'

'Oh dear. I don't take any notice of all that Internet stuff, but I should inform the police, shouldn't I? Or should I check with the vicar first — what do you think?'

'Yes, you should call the police and ask them if you can file a report. That way, they'll have all the information on record if someone informs them they have your missing puppy. Or, if you hear she's been spotted, you can quote the crime number then. After that, we should contact the pet recovery service and let any local animal shelters know.'

Susie took out a large white handkerchief and mopped her eyes. Blew her nose. 'I feel as if all the stuffing's gone out of me, I really do, erm — sorry, my head's spinning. For the moment I've forgotten your name.'

'It's Hannah Ross. I only know yours because Mrs Ferguson called at the shop this morning. She'd forgotten to buy rice milk for the vicar, so that's what I was doing here. I put the carton in the fridge, by the way. I'm also delivering flyers, warning dog owners to — um, be very careful with their pets.'

Susie burst into tears. 'I'm cracking up, Hannah. How am I going to break this news to the vicar?'

Hannah put her arms around Susie and hugged her. 'You're definitely not cracking up. You've had a dreadful shock. I'm going to pour you a cup of strong tea and stir some sugar into it. Afterwards, you can speak to the police and I'll be right beside you.'

'I don't know the number of the local station. But I shouldn't ring 999, should I?'

'Good thinking, Susie. See — I told you you're not cracking up. If you dial 101, you'll reach someone who'll help you.'

Hannah felt nobody, unless they possessed a heart of stone, could blame Susie for reacting as she did. She was on the verge of weeping with her too. What a fiasco of a morning this had turned out to be. Despite all the warnings, another dog had been whisked from under someone's nose, and might already be miles away from Bailsford.

9

Hannah rang her grandfather, and also sent a text to Ryan as soon as she left the vicarage. Ryan rang back immediately.

'Hi, should I come over to yours?'

'Better still, could you meet me at Granddad's? I'm on my way there now. We need a committee meeting.'

'Whose dog has gone missing?'

'One of the vicarage dog's pups. Sasha's little Juliet.'

Ryan groaned. 'She's a Llasa Apso. My mother's been talking about them. They're pricey to buy so I guess a good breed to steal from a crook's point of view.'

'Whatever the breed, it's still awful for the owners,' said Hannah.

'Have you seen them at all?'

'The vicar and his wife don't even know she's been taken yet.' Hannah explained what had happened. 'I'm outside my granddad's cottage now. See you in a bit?'

'Yeah. Hey, have you had lunch yet, with all that going on?'

'Nope. I went straight from the shop to the vicarage. What about you?'

'Not. I'll bring us a snack from the kitchen. Mum'll sort it.'

Before Hannah could protest, he closed the call. She pushed open the side gate and made her way to the back door. Rapped and opened it far enough to call through.

'Come in, darling,' Greg Ross called.

She found him seated at the kitchen table, blue-and-white-striped coffee mug alongside his laptop. He held a pen in one hand and was using the other one to carry out some speedy two-finger typing.

He peered at her over the top of his specs. 'This is extremely bad news, Hannah. Come and sit down. Have you eaten?'

'Everyone's very concerned about my

food intake today. Actually, Ryan's coming round in a bit, Granddad. He said he'd bring something to eat. I hope that's all right?'

'Of course. I've taken cheese and tomatoes from the fridge so we can have a Ploughman's. If he's bringing more food, we shall have a veritable feast.'

'It seems awful, planning what to eat when we know that sweet little puppy's been stolen by some despicable person who took advantage of someone's good nature.'

'I know. But a successful army marches on its stomach, my girl. Or something like that.'

She smiled at him. 'In other words, we need to keep up our strength.'

'Well, yes. We need to gather all the facts about this latest disappearance. Check for similarities with the first one. Ask around people we know in areas outside Bailsford to see if anything's been happening on their patch. Thanks to my cricket club contacts, I can start on that this afternoon. You said Susie rang the police?'

'I waited while she spoke to them. She's devastated, of course. Kept saying how she wished she'd closed the door in that woman's face so she couldn't set foot inside. So, what are you writing down now? Don't we know all the things we need to do after what happened last time?'

'Yes, but I'm making a more comprehensive list of places we need to ring or email about this latest theft, like the local dog warden and some vet practices. I found a very useful website offering suggestions we didn't think of regarding the Andrews' lost pet.'

'Okay. Brilliant.' She glanced up and saw a figure cross the window. 'There's Ryan now.'

'Come in, young Ryan,' called Greg. 'My stomach thinks my throat's been cut, so I'm about to demolish some bread and cheese.'

Hannah closed the door behind Ryan.

He held out a carrier bag. 'Mum sent these. They're still warm.'

His hand brushed against Hannah's as she took the bag from him, and she felt a surge of happiness totally unrelated to the prospect of food.

'Or shall I be Mum?' Ryan's eyes twinkled.

Hannah handed the carrier back to him. 'Go on, then. You dish them out while I find cutlery and pour us some water. Granddad, can you bring Ryan up to speed with what you've found out, please?'

'It's more about our strategy than the circumstances of this theft, my boy. My list of people and organisations we should contact has grown since I researched the first time.'

'Awesome.' Ryan headed towards the kitchen counter and took out a plastic container that Hannah could see contained a colourful salad. He then produced a foil-wrapped package.

'I can see the plates from here,' he said. 'Perhaps I can interest you in a warm chicken and mushroom pasty before your bread and cheese?'

Greg chuckled. 'Your mother's pasties are already legendary amongst the cognoscenti, young Ryan. Many thanks.' He turned to Hannah. 'I think you should explain exactly what the vicarage housekeeper told you when you arrived this morning. I'll make notes while we eat.'

'Yum,' said Hannah. 'I feel a bit guilty, tucking into your mother's brilliant bar food, Ryan. I certainly shan't need bread and cheese after one of her pasties. How about I make her a cake, now I've had one go at that lovely chocolate recipe?'

She saw his face light up. 'She bakes, but no one ever makes a cake for her! But you're going to be busy, what with the shop and now all this dog stuff, so please don't feel you have to, young Hannah.'

She waved her hand in front of his face, pretending to be outraged.

'Hah,' said Greg, looking up. 'Point taken. I really must stop calling you young Ryan; and in turn, you must call me Greg and not Mr Ross.'

'Cool,' said Ryan. 'Maybe we should have a name for our team of super-sleuths. What d'you think? Dogs 'R' Us? Dog Whisperers?'

'I'm hopeless at thinking up names,' said Hannah.

'Whether we have a name or not, one thing is certain,' said Greg.

'What's that?' Hannah asked.

'Unless the perpetrators of this appalling theft contact the vicarage soon to dictate terms for a ransom, I think we can take it that, as with the first disappearance, we definitely don't have a dog-napping on our hands.'

* * *

'Doesn't it seem sad, having to take a second poster round so people can see there's another dog gone missing?'

'It does,' said Ryan. 'But it's important we spread the news as soon as possible. I take it the lady who works at the vicarage has heard nothing about the puppy?'

'Susie promised to ring my mobile if she heard anything, but so far she hasn't been in touch.'

The pair were sitting in Greg Ross's garden while he put his feet up and took a nap. Hannah looked up at blue fragments of summer sky peeping through little gaps in the bright green foliage above their heads.

Ryan was first to break the silence, apart from the birdsong in the background. 'I like your granddad's suggestion that we could try a crime scene reconstruction.'

'I noticed you sit up when he said that,' said Hannah. 'He does watch a lot of TV detective dramas though, and I'm not sure what good it'll do. Presupposing the vicar gives us permission.'

'Shall we call at the vicarage later and ask him?'

'Poor man. This is going to come as a shock, especially as Susie's likely to burst into tears when she breaks the news.'

'Maybe she'd like you there with her. I could wait on the green for you if you think that's best. He won't have a clue who I am.'

'You'd be surprised.' Hannah longed to suggest that surely Ryan had met the vicar during the time he was hanging out with Mr Ferguson's daughter, but thought better of it. 'Granddad told me the vicar enjoys a pint after the cricket match. I bet he knows exactly who you are — and don't forget, your folks are always very generous about donating prizes for raffles and so on.'

She noticed Ryan's surprised expression.

'Are they? I never thought about it. I did hand over a painting to them once for something or other, but I can't remember what it was all about.'

Hannah burst out laughing. 'Some lucky person must have an original Ryan Hawkins hanging on his or her wall. You really do possess the artistic personality — creative and all that. Sometimes you seem deep in a world of your own.' She paused. 'Somewhere I can't follow.'

He turned to her. Took one of her hands in both of his. Raised it to his lips and kissed her fingertips.

'Oh.' She caught her breath as she saw the tenderness in his eyes. Saw him gazing at her mouth.

'I would very much like to kiss you,' he said. 'But only if that's what you'd like too, Hannah.'

A sweet, floral scent wafted from the climbing roses on the wall. Her heart suddenly seemed to have upped its rhythm. Still he held on to her hand. She wanted to be kissed, of course she wanted to be kissed, but a part of her worried about shattering the precious and still-fledgling friendship they'd established. Did she really want their relationship to change gear so soon? Weren't he and she fine as they were, especially with two dog thefts clouding the sensational summer's day and so much to do?

She could sense him waiting. This wasn't some awkward young boy she was sitting next to on her granddad's garden bench. She knew Ryan would be celebrating his twenty-first birthday before they started their uni courses. He was gorgeous. She felt as thought she'd fallen into one of those time-standing-still moments. What was wrong with her? Why was she so frightened of showing her feelings?

'Hannah?'

She looked straight at him. His eyes would surely require a shade of dreamy Mediterranean blue if he or some other artist had to paint them. She could see the thick, black lashes. She caught a whiff of soap or shower gel. Lemony. Sharp. Tangy. Her gaze took in his chin, with no sign of stubble, let alone a scruffy almost-beard like Ben's friend, Jack Russell's.

She noticed Ryan's lips twitch. 'Maybe you're afraid of my bristly chin?

I did shave this morning, you know.'

He'd broken the ice. Hannah laughed.

'You have such a fabulous laugh,' he said. 'You're so lovely, Hannah.'

She put both arms around him. Leaned in. This time, her lips found his, rather than his cheek. She closed her eyes. Felt his arms tighten around her as delicious tingles made her wish the moment could last forever.

After their first very big, very satisfactory kiss, she'd been up on Cloud Nine. But after this latest one, she knew she wanted Ryan for her boyfriend. Being mates was great. But now they'd kissed — really kissed — again, she couldn't care less about what might or mightn't happen in the autumn when they both left for different universities. Maybe this would be a holiday romance. Maybe it would fizzle out as swiftly as it started. Maybe it would lead to something deeper. But just at that moment, with her Prince Charming's arms around her and the birds making background music straight from a Walt Disney movie, Hannah felt very happy.

They broke apart at the sound of a loud harrumphing. Ryan scrambled to his feet and held out his hand to Hannah. She rose and stood beside him, feeling exactly as she'd felt years before, when her granddad, babysitting her, had caught her raiding her mum's tin of expensive chocolate biscuits.

Greg stood outside the back door, beaming at them and peering over the top of his specs as usual. 'Sorry to interrupt you lovebirds, but I'd like to run through a few things, if that's in order.'

Hannah, still holding Ryan's hand, followed her grandfather back inside. Ryan pulled out Greg's big chair at the head of the long table, and he and Hannah sat down opposite him. Hannah loved the way Ryan reached over and took her hand back in his, but under Greg's radar this time.

'I won't keep you long,' said her granddad. 'But I do want to establish something before we begin publicising this second dog theft.'

'We're listening,' said Ryan.

'Hannah, you've described how distraught Susie was. Are we quite sure she didn't become confused and agree for this smartly-dressed lady to take away the puppy for a trial visit to her home?'

Hannah frowned. 'I'm positive. She'd never do that, not in a million years. Besides, even if this Sheila McCarthy had coaxed her into agreeing to a trial period, surely Susie would have asked for some kind of ID and taken contact details. She's been fielding messages for the vicar for many years now, not just cleaning the house and doing the laundry.'

'I'm aware of that, Hannah,' said Greg, 'And Susie is a lovely woman, but she's very trusting as well as honest as the day is long. I know I'm probably on the wrong track here, but you understand that we have to explore all the 'what if's?'

'Greg's right,' said Ryan. 'I think,

now Susie has had several hours to calm down and think back to what happened, it might be good to have another chat with her.'

He looked at Greg. 'I've suggested Hannah might ring, or call on Susie again, and — with her permission, of course — wait with her for the vicar to come home so Susie doesn't find it too daunting to break the bad news. Not that the vicar's intimidating, of course,' he said quickly.

'Good idea. If our dear vicar will allow it, we can carry out our reconstruction based on information provided. I'm afraid, Ryan, if we do this, either you or I will have to take a female role in the proceedings.'

Ryan stared at him. 'Yes, of course. One housekeeper, one female puppy snatcher, and one accomplice waiting in the wings.'

'On second thoughts,' said Greg, 'Maybe Susie should be part of this. She could retrace her own footsteps. One of us will ring the vicarage from our mobile and she can have a chat or say goodbye and count to thirty before she goes back to the study.'

'Don't forget, the hidden accomplice might also be female.' Hannah looked from one to the other. 'All our suspicions of Jack Russell are pure supposition at the moment. We need to keep an open mind.'

Greg pushed his chunky notepad across the table. 'Yes, we must never fall into the trap of jumping into conclusions. Have a look at my list, and tell me what you think about the last question I've posed concerning Juliet's theft.'

Ryan read the curly black script aloud. '*Has the person we know as Jack Russell ever visited the vicarage and been given a job to do that might involve him entering the house and learning the lie of the land?*'

He looked up. 'Sorry, what does 'lie of the land' mean, please?'

Hannah giggled and tried to turn it into a cough.

Greg sighed. 'What do they teach you youngsters nowadays? Its actual meaning is to establish the shape and contour of the land under consideration; doubtless, back in the mists of antiquity, it was vital in terms of a military manoeuvre or battle.'

'So, like 'case the joint'?'

'If you insist. Though it does sound rather like a line from a *New Tricks* or *EastEnders* script, young Ryan.'

Ryan held up his free hand. '*New Tricks* is cool, but 'young Ryan'? Yellow card, Greg!'

'I'm sorry. Let's get back to the agenda, shall we?'

Ryan nodded. 'Okay. I know where you're coming from.'

Hannah glanced at her granddad to see if he showed signs of being wound up.

'Cool,' he said. And sat back in his chair, arms folded across his jolly woolly jumper, as he liked to describe it.

Hannah shook her head. 'What are

you two like? I think you've made a good point though, Granddad. I went to the vicarage once with Jodie.' She avoided looking at Ryan. 'The mums-and-toddlers group had to meet there because the village hall was being redecorated. That house was busier than I ever dreamt it would be.'

'How do you mean?' Ryan frowned. 'By the way, I never got an invitation to visit.'

Hannah decided not to comment.

'Our vicar is in charge of three parishes,' said Greg. 'He's a busy man.'

'Well, the phone never stopped ringing,' Hannah continued. 'While Mr Ferguson was talking to Jodie and me in the kitchen, he left the door open, and I could hear someone — probably Susie — answering calls. The mothers and children were upstairs in the old nursery, but one or two mums came down to mix a jug of orange squash and make coffee.'

'And Bailsford Church is a particu-larly pretty one with a traditional lychgate, so it attracts inquiries from people wishing to be married there — which I find very heartening, considering this bizarre age in which we live,' said Greg.

'Okay,' said Ryan. 'Hannah, could you ask Susie whether she could possibly have misled Sheila McCarthy into thinking it was all right to take the puppy home for a short period?'

'I'll ask, but I bet she'll be horrified.'

'What about our friendly odd-job man? Could you ask her about him too, or ask the vicar maybe?'

'Susie probably knows more about the day-to-day running of the vicarage than its incumbent does,' said Greg.

'While I think of it, can you tell me why there doesn't seem to be any maintenance man or whatever in Bailsford?' Ryan raised his dark eyebrows at Greg.

'Ah, well, there used to be a chap living in the old farm cottages but he retired a few months back and went to live with his daughter in Gloucester.'

'So that's the reason why Jack Russell has been picking up repair jobs recently? There's no one else around to ask.'

'Absolutely. Specialists like thatchers and chimney sweeps and boiler engineers come in from wherever, but when it's a case of simple repair jobs, elderly people especially find it difficult to obtain help.'

'And don't forget very busy people,' said Hannah.

'Plus the favoured few who own holiday homes here,' said Ryan. 'They come into The Seven Stars at weekends, and it's done a lot to help trade, but I know some people are a tad resentful of them.'

'That's village life in a nutshell,' said Greg. 'So, is that all? Everybody happy?'

'I'll be happier if we can stop any more dogs being stolen,' said Hannah.

'And happier still if we can find the whereabouts of Toffee and Juliet,' said Greg.

Ryan rose and went over to the worktop to collect his food bag, empty but for the plastic container. 'So, if the vicar's up for it, we all agree we should carry out the crime reconstruction as soon as possible?'

10

Hannah parted company with Ryan, who'd promised to cut the grass in The Seven Stars' leisure area. She walked back to Manor View, her mind rerunning the events of the morning and the discussion afterwards. But most of all, her thoughts lingered on Ryan. He'd rushed back home saying he wanted to get his chores done and jump in the shower before he called to pick her up at six and walk her to the vicarage.

She let herself into the house she'd left neat and tidy only that morning. It seemed as though several days had passed instead of six hours or so. Ryan hadn't mentioned wanting to spend time with her after she spoke to Susie and consulted the vicar. Would he want to go out somewhere? Or should she ask him to supper?

What a dilemma! Dating one special young man hadn't figured in her lifestyle so far. Friendships with boys had been casual in her schooldays. For a moment, she thought of Ben again, and how he'd kissed her that summer beneath the willow tree. That moment had seemed a landmark back then; but now she'd shared such special kisses with Ryan, she realised how much more significant they were than that one in her young teenage days. To be fair, she'd tried to act grown up, as Ben had. That brief conversation with him outside her house had soon proved to her that the almost-adult Ben wasn't someone she wanted to spend time with.

Not like Ryan. Hannah longed to know more about Ryan: about his childhood, his memories — particularly those of boarding school. He'd asked to be sent away there. Hannah would never, ever have considered such a thing. But in his case, he obviously didn't want to face any more moving on, and the packing and unpacking involved when his dad was ordered to yet another posting.

In the kitchen, she opened the fridge and inspected the contents of the salad crisper, finding a couple of onions. In the main compartment she'd left two chicken breasts to defrost. She checked the food cupboard and found a container of risotto rice. Olive oil — trust her mum to buy the expensive green sort — stood in a tall bottle near the electric cooker.

Hannah unlocked the back door and crossed the patio to check out the herb garden. It hadn't dried out after all the sunshine that day, and she decided to use the plant that gave out a lemony fragrance when she rubbed one of its leaves between her fingers. She wasn't sure about the white wine. Maybe she'd use chicken stock instead.

But was it too soon to offer to cook supper for Ryan? What if he thought she was trying her hardest to impress him? Maybe baked beans on toast would be more appropriate.

She shook her head and went indoors to place the sprigs of herb in water. She might be wasting her time if what he intended was to get back home and help his folks that evening.

She could always share the meal with her granddad next day. Hannah took a deep breath and headed upstairs to take a shower.

★ ★ ★

She saw Ryan waiting for her when she turned the corner and walked towards the green. He was sitting on the grass, focusing his camera on a duck. *No change there, then*, she thought as she loped towards him.

'You're wearing a frock!' He stood up and tucked his camera into his jeans pocket.

'Top marks for observation,' she teased.

'I like you in frocks, but is this one for the vicar's benefit or mine?' He put his arm around her waist and they

191

started walking towards the vicarage.

'I didn't want to turn up in my shorts and T-shirt.'

'I see. So the pretty dress with the daisies on is to impress the vicar. That's probably a good idea. Can't win 'em all.' He squeezed her close.

No way had she stopped those adolescent blushes. Hannah felt her cheeks grow warm, but Ryan's attitude towards her made her feel happy. Secure. Excited. And, at the same time, just a tiny bit scared.

'Can we spend the whole evening together? Dad's given me a Get Out Of Jail Free card.'

'I'd like that,' she said. 'How about I make risotto?'

'At Rose Cottage?'

'No, knucklehead,' she laughed. 'At Number Eleven — just the two of us.'

For a moment, she wondered if she sounded what her remaining grandma would surely describe as 'fast'. But Ryan didn't seem to find anything wrong with her statement.

'Cool,' he said. 'But why don't I help you?'

They stopped at the open gates of the vicarage.

'Here we go then,' said Hannah. 'Wish me luck?'

'Break a leg,' he said. 'It'll be fine. I think I'll go for a wander in the churchyard. I keep meaning to do that.'

'Well, it's good to know you have such a fascinating hobby.'

He looked down at her, his eyes sparkling with fun. 'Off you go,' he said. 'I truly won't be far away. But I have to take photos of those awesome stone angels. I keep seeing that *Doctor Who* sequence.'

'In other words, you feel a picture coming on.'

She watched him set off towards the ancient wrought-iron gates of the churchyard, turning to give her a wave as she walked towards the yellow-brick Georgian house, home to a long line of rural vicars for decades before the

Ferguson family moved in, continuing the tradition.

Susie came to the door almost immediately.

'Me again, I'm afraid. I hope I'm not intruding,' said Hannah.

'Not at all,' said Susie. 'Come in. I'm just waiting for the vicar to get back, and I'm not looking forward to his reaction.'

Hannah joined her in the flagstoned hallway. 'I can imagine. That's why I'm here. I can wait in the kitchen, or I can hold your hand, whichever you prefer.'

Before Susie could answer, Hannah heard the sound of tyres crunching over gravel.

'He's here! Oh my, he must've managed to get away early. Oh, Hannah, yes, stay with me please, in case I burst into tears and make a fool of myself.'

'I doubt you'll ever do that, but if it all gets too much, just give me a nod and I'll do my best to fill in the facts for him. Now, how about we sit on that lovely old pew under the window, so we don't look too much like a reception committee? And please don't look so worried. I doubt very much he'll blame you for what's happened.'

★ ★ ★

'What did he say? How did you get on?' Ryan emerged from behind a towering lichen-covered monument as Hannah stood on the gravelled path, looking around for him.

'Phew, I'm glad it's broad daylight. For a moment there I thought I was meeting the Phantom of the Opera.'

'I knew I should've worn my mask and cloak. So, what did he say, Hannah? In your own time, of course.'

'As I thought, he wasn't in the least angry with Susie. He's a lovely man and, as I tried to tell her, he thinks the world of her, that's perfectly obvious. She had a little weep, but he took out a bottle of sherry from a cupboard in his study and got her to drink a half-glass.

He's driving her home now.'

'Did you get to ask him what he thought of our plan?'

'Oh, yes. He was curious as to why I was there, but very grateful to us for our interest. He's a big fan of Granddad's, of course, so that probably clinched the deal. He looked a bit bemused when I mentioned Jack Russell, then said he must have been the chap to whom his wife gave the job of cleaning all the downstairs windows.'

Ryan's face lit up. 'Everyone knows window cleaners get a bird's-eye view of house interiors, even if only the ground floor. He could've learnt a lot while he was doing that job. There must be at least half a dozen rooms needing their windows cleaned.'

'The big sitting room also has French windows.'

'He could even have gone inside for a cup of tea or to use the downstairs cloakroom. I bet we're on the right track.' He punched the air. 'So we're on for tomorrow?'

'We are,' said Hannah. 'Mr Ferguson's visiting one of his parishioners in hospital tomorrow morning but Susie will be in, so it's agreed I should ring the bell at ten o'clock and she'll follow the same pattern as she did earlier today when that woman called.'

'Excellent. Although I was quite looking forward to seeing Greg in a dress.'

Hannah shook her head at him. 'You're mad as a March hare, Ryan Hawkins. Do you know that?'

'All I know is, I'm mad about you, Hannah Ross.' He lifted her up in his arms and whirled her round.

She managed to stop herself squealing in protest. 'Bad boy. You should be more respectful.'

He returned her to earth and made a contrite face. 'Yes, I'm sorry. That was thoughtless of me, I appreciate that.'

They walked in silence down a grassy strip between rows of weathered tombstones.

'My grandma's plot is over the other

side,' said Hannah.

Ryan put his arm round her shoulders and squeezed her to him. 'I could kick myself for doing such a naff thing.'

'She would probably have laughed. Gran-Gran was lovely, and she'd have been thrilled to see us happy.'

'And she's laid to rest in a fantastic place, close to her loved ones, isn't she?'

Hannah felt taken aback. This boy was all contrasts and you couldn't help loving him. Well, she couldn't, anyway.

'Just look at this.' Ryan indicated a large headstone to their left. 'That's a story in itself. See the inscription? *Mary Clay, 1885–1919*. Mary left behind a husband, George and three children. The widower and two of the children are there too. I wonder what happened to the third child.' He counted aloud. 'That last one could even be still alive.'

Hannah shivered. 'I agree it's fascinating, Ryan, but I think we should go home now. I don't know about you, but I'm feeling totally shattered.'

'Then how about you sit back and

watch me prepare our dinner?'

'Are you seriously telling me you can cook as well as wait at tables and create fabulous paintings? How inadequate is that supposed to make me feel?'

He pulled her through the open gates and stood facing her, holding both her hands. 'That's just plain silly. I was only trying to be helpful.'

She felt a moment of panic. Had she upset him? He sounded a bit defensive. But to her relief he grabbed her hand and the two of them set off in the direction of Manor View.

'You forgot to mention my grass-cutting talents,' he said.

Hannah tweaked his ear, and they chatted and bickered about crazy skills like making daisy chains and skimming pebbles and which of them could do better than the other all the way home.

★ ★ ★

Next morning, Hannah dressed in the same primrose-colour skirt suit she'd worn to collect her exam certificates in London at her school Speech Day. It wasn't that long ago, but already seemed ages. She tucked her shoulder-length hair into a scrunchy and applied a little make-up to her face before pushing her feet into a pair of high-heeled sandals.

She slipped her mobile phone into her jacket pocket and put on a pair of sunglasses, surveying herself in her mum's full-length mirror before going downstairs to pick up her cream leather shoulder bag.

As she turned out of Manor View, she stopped in her tracks. Outside a thatched cottage, where the village cricket captain and his wife lived, stood the grubby white van belonging to Jack Russell. Her heart beat a bit faster. She wanted to tell Ryan, but also wanted to take a photo so she had the van plus its registration number on her phone. The odd-job man might even be sitting inside his vehicle if he'd just arrived. She continued walking, trying to look as though her tummy wasn't turning somersaults, and let her breath out in a whoosh at the sight of the empty driving seat.

The thatch topping of the cricket captain's cottage always reminded Hannah of a dog's shaggy coat. More importantly, near the front door stood a thick bush springing from the grass verge; and here Hannah paused, bending over as if trying to get rid of a stitch in her side. She pulled out her phone, making quite sure no one was sitting in the van before taking a photograph.

She stayed where she was to text Ryan — who, she thought must surely have arrived at the vicarage. Her thoughts were in turmoil. If Jack Russell really was involved in the dog thefts, surely he couldn't risk returning to the village again? Wouldn't he move on somewhere else to continue his disreputable trade? But her granddad wouldn't necessarily agree with her. There were so many loose ends!

She saw her granddad sitting on a bench overlooking the duck pond as she rounded the next bend in the road. He was reading his newspaper, or appeared to be doing so, and looked up as she approached across the grass.

'Morning, darling,' he said. 'You scrub up well. I've just spoken to that boyfriend of yours. You'll find him lurking inside the churchyard.'

She smiled. 'He seems to find lots to interest him in there. Did he tell you whose van I just spotted up the road?'

'Indeed he did.' Greg checked his watch. 'Better get moving. Now, remember, I'm just here to observe. The rest is down to you two, and maybe you'll come back and let me know how it went after you've done the deed.'

'Sure we will. See you in a bit.'

Hannah headed for the churchyard. She saw Ryan walking down the path towards her, and they met outside the vicarage gates. He leaned in and kissed her cheek. 'Good morning, Hannah.

Thanks again for a brilliant dinner last night.'

'It was a joint effort. Why so formal?'

'We're on important business here, Miss Ross. No time for passionate embraces.'

'I should think not, indeed; especially as I'm a married woman this morning.'

'So you are. Thanks for the text. Finding Jack Russell's van in the village is very interesting.'

'I think it's either very brazen, or else he really is a repair man and we're barking up the wrong tree, if you'll pardon the pun.'

'Yeah.' Ryan looked a little disconsolate. 'You'd better go do your thing. I've taken a look at the flowerbed outside the study window and there's no sign of any footprints. Mind you, with so many weeds around the thingamajig flowers, you can't actually see the earth.'

'A gold star for thinking of doing it anyway,' said Hannah. 'At least I shan't be destroying any expensive plants when I climb through the window.'

'I'll give you two minutes after Susie lets you in, then I'll ring the vicarage number. OK?'

'Perfect.'

Hannah headed straight to the front door. She pushed the bell and waited until she heard footsteps in the hallway and the door opened wide.

'Good morning,' said Hannah quickly. She took off her sunglasses and gave Susie a big smile. 'Mrs Ferguson? I wonder if it's convenient for me to have a look at the puppies you're selling?'

'I'm afraid Mrs Ferguson's not at home.'

'Oh, dear.' Hannah frowned. 'What a disappointment. I suppose I should've rung ahead, but I only just heard from a friend that there were puppies for sale at Bailsford Vicarage and I couldn't resist coming straight over. I've always wanted to own a Lhasa, um, Apso, and, um, well, that's about it really.'

'Would you like to give me your name and address? I'll need to take contact details for the vicar. I'm sure he'll ring you tonight and arrange a time for you to call back.'

'Okay. I'm Sheila McCarthy, and it's Mrs. Could you let me have a pen and paper, please?'

'I'll show you into the study Mr Ferguson uses to talk to his parishioners,' said Susie, leading the way. Inside the room she tore off a sheet from the notepad on the vicar's desk and handed Hannah, also known as Mrs McCarthy, a pen.

'Thanks.'

Susie crossed to the window. 'I'll just let in a little fresh air.'

Hannah grimaced. 'I could kick myself for not ringing first. My husband will be so cross with me for wasting petrol.'

Susie blinked hard. 'Do you know what? I think I may as well go and fetch one puppy at a time so you can have a quick peep now you're here. I can't see why my employers would object, and the mum dog won't make a fuss because she's used to me being around.

I helped Mrs Ferguson when Sasha was giving birth to her babies.'

'Fantastic. Good for you.' The bogus Mrs McCarthy smiled. 'It's kind of you to let me have a peep. I guess the pups are old enough to leave their mum now?'

'Definitely. The first two have already gone to a good home.'

'That's nice. And if I fall in love with one of the last pair, he or she will be looked after well, too.' Hannah hesitated. 'Oh, yes, I meant to say I left my car parked on the road outside the vicarage for fear of leaving it in someone's way. Is it all right there?'

'Fine. I'll be back in two ticks.'

Hannah watched Susie hurry away before scribbling *Mrs Sheila McCarthy, 14 New Road, Starsbrook*, followed by a row of Xs to represent a mobile phone number. She stood up straight and waited for Susie to return. The housekeeper hurried back across the wide hallway and entered the study, carrying a rolled-up kitchen towel in her arms. Hannah waited for her to come closer.

'Oh, what a sweetheart.'

'I'll put her down on the floor for you,' said Susie.

Hannah dropped to her knees. Susie placed the towel on the carpet and straightened up while Hannah made the right noises.

As Susie moved towards the window and opened it, Hannah waited for the hall phone to ring.

★　★　★

Ryan, waiting while seconds ticked by, was positioned within sight of the vicarage. He kept Greg in view but he wasn't prepared to see Jack Russell's dilapidated van proceed slowly down the road and turn into the vicarage driveway.

What was all that about? Ryan couldn't afford to hang around if they were to go ahead with this reconstruction. He could no longer see the van because of the curve of the driveway, but he called up the number as planned. It didn't take long for Susie to answer.

'It's me, Ryan. I'm not going to give you a sales pitch, so I'll rely on you to close the call, like we agreed.'

'Good. Yes, that's fine. I remembered to open the window, and Hannah's now alone in the study.'

'The thing is — ' Ryan hesitated. 'I can't see from where I'm standing, but that white van belonging to the guy who's been doing odd jobs in the village just drove through your gateway. He must be parked outside right now. I'm not sure how this might affect Hannah.'

'He's probably come to tout for another job,' said Susie. 'I'm not sure what to do, either. What if he sees her climbing through the window?'

'With a rolled-up towel tucked inside her jacket? She's going to look a bit silly.'

'Shall I go and stop her?'

'I think you'll have to. What a pain.'

Susie closed the call. She whizzed across the hallway and burst into the study, only to find the bird already flown. She poked her head through the window and saw no sign of Hannah, who'd obviously followed Plan A and must be on her way to meet Ryan. The van she recognised as belonging to the odd-job man was parked under a copper beech tree to one side of the forecourt.

A loud shriek erupted from some-where, an enraged yell that made Susie jump with shock. She hurried towards the front door and opened it. 'Hannah? Are you all right?' She shouted as loudly as she could but no one answered.

Susie, confident she'd left the two remaining pets safely shut in the kitchen — and still proud of being the only school mum to win the annual village school Sports Day mothers' race three years in succession — took off down the driveway.

Hannah, Ryan and the odd-job man,

whose name Susie couldn't recall, were standing in the strangest of tableaux. Ryan had the odd-job man in what appeared to be a stranglehold, while Hannah was yelling at both of them.

'Stop it! All of you, please stop shouting at once.' Susie came to a halt and bent over, hands on her knees, clearly out of puff.

Hannah went over to her. 'Gosh, are you okay, Susie? I never thought you could run like that.'

'I heard — phew — it was you screaming that did it, Hannah. What's going on?'

'Maybe you should ask him?' Hannah pointed at a very puzzled-looking Jack Russell.

'Hello?'

At the sound of the new voice, everyone looked at Greg Ross, who'd rounded the driveway.

'What's the commotion?' Greg held his mobile phone up. 'Should I call for help?'

'Please,' said Jack Russell. 'I caught

this young lady trying to make her getaway after climbing through one of the vicarage windows.' He scowled at Ryan. 'Give me a break, mate, and let go of me. I'm not going anywhere — though *you* might be.'

*   *   *

'I'm pleased you had nothing to do with either of the dog thefts, Jack,' said Hannah, accepting a custard cream biscuit from the plate Susie was offering to her four visitors. The dogs were snoozing, curled up together on an ancient armchair by the range, and Susie had offered her guests some early elevenses.

'My mum keeps telling me to smarten myself up. I can't blame you for thinking I might be a bit suss.'

'When Mrs Warner said you'd asked if she had a dog, I latched onto that. Stupid of me, of course,' said Hannah.

'Aha,' said Jack. 'I always ask that question so I'm prepared. I'd hate someone's dog to get at an open can of paint, for more than one reason.'

Hannah remembered the Andrews' neighbour suggesting something similar. 'I can't apologise enough.' She made a contrite face at Jack. 'We even decided your name was made up!'

'Yeah, sorry mate. I guess we put two and two together and made seven and a half,' said Ryan. 'Our decision to go for a crime reconstruction seemed a good idea in theory, but it just goes to show: split-second timing's very important.'

'I don't think your timing was the fly in the ointment,' said Greg. 'Mr Russell here happened to come along out of the blue and dropped a spanner in the works so Hannah ended up caught like a deer in the headlights.'

'How many metaphors can you mix in one sentence?' Jack Russell burst out laughing. 'I'm sorry, Mr Ross. I shouldn't be so impertinent. Please forgive me.'

Hannah exchanged glances with Ryan. This guy had hidden depths. Her granddad was looking very impressed.

'My word, young Jack, you're a fellow after my own heart.'

Hannah didn't dare look at Ryan. Whoever would have thought the morning would progress as it was?

'Yeah, I'm pleased as well that you're not the baddy, Jack,' said Ryan. 'But we're still no closer to solving the problem. Plus we've got loads of flyers to push through letterboxes and social media stuff to get on with.'

'I'm very grateful for your efforts,' said Susie, who'd sat down and kept twisting a pink-and-white handkerchief between her fingers. 'The vicar will be pleased, too. I know he has some garden chores he'd be glad for you to take on.'

Jack's face brightened. 'Ace. I'm calling on people I've worked for previously, hoping they'll give me something else to do. Going to uni costs megabucks. I can't wait to be qualified and start working so my mum can give up doing night shifts.'

Hannah closed her eyes briefly and vowed to herself never, ever, again to judge someone on the basis of their appearance. Hadn't she scolded Ryan for doing that very thing when he'd scoffed at the idea of Ben's friend being interested in the church?

Ryan cleared this throat. 'What are you studying?'

'Sports Science at Loughborough. I do some shifts at a local supermarket during term-time. If all goes well and I get my degree next year, I'm prepared to work anywhere I can find the right job. My younger sister still lives at home, so my mother has company when I'm not around.'

He turned to Ryan. 'Tell you what, mate, if you let me have some of those flyers, I can hand them out or stuff them through letterboxes while I'm doing my calls.'

'Cool.' Ryan grinned at him.

'Much appreciated, young Jack.' Greg nodded his head.

Hannah looked at the kitchen clock.

'Susie, we mustn't hold you up any longer. Thanks for the drinks and everything. I'm going to take these guys back to my house so we can share out posters and stuff; but before we go, I have something to show you. It may mean nothing, but it could be a clue leading us to the woman calling herself Mrs McCarthy.'

'So this morning's efforts may not all have been in vain?'

Hannah smiled, and placed something small and sparkly on the table.

11

'Yes, well, I wanted to make sure we'd cleared things up — about your being in the village, I mean, Jack. And I have to say, the people I questioned about you were very quick to praise your work.'

'Really? Thanks, Hannah.' Jack smiled at her across the table. 'You've made my day.'

'Let's have a look?' Ryan leaned forward.

Hannah hoped he didn't think she was trying to flirt with Jack Russell. She hesitated. 'Susie, could you spare an empty matchbox or something, please? We should all take a look at this earring, but I'm afraid to let it jiggle around in my pocket. It looks expensive to me, but I'm no expert.'

'I have just the thing.' Susie crossed over to the big dresser and opened one of the drawers. 'Mrs Ferguson hoards all kinds of oddments in here. I'm sure she wouldn't mind you having this ring box.'

'Perfect. There you are, Ryan. What d'you think of that?'

He held the jewellery up so the sunlight streaming through the kitchen window set the red stone on fire.

'Wow,' he said. 'My guess is that it's a ruby, set in diamonds, same as my mother's engagement ring. No way does Mum have any earrings like this, though.'

Greg leaned across. 'May I?' He peered at the earring. 'I'd go along with that, Ryan. Those stones don't look like fakes to me. How about young Jack here? Are you an expert?'

Jack chuckled. 'No, sir, I'm pretty clueless over that sort of thing. Could I take a closer look, though?'

'You could indeed.' Greg handed over the box.

'Sentimental value might come into it too,' said Susie, looking over Jack's shoulder. 'I agree it looks like a valuable piece. I'd be gutted if I lost an earring like that.'

'Absolutely,' said Jack. 'It's certainly beautiful. And it occurs to me — if you're right, which I suspect you are, it must be worth a fair bit of money.'

'And your point is?' Ryan looked at him.

'It could be a wild goose chase, but whoever's lost this might try and recover it. If indeed it does belong to the woman you've told me about.' He handed the box back to Hannah.

'Where exactly did you find it?' Greg asked.

'It must've fallen off while the woman was making her escape with little Juliet. When I looked down to make sure I didn't land on anything dodgy, I saw something glittering. Because I wasn't trying to break the world record for escaping through a ground-floor window, I stopped to pick up the earring. It was sitting on top of the earth in a flowerpot.'

'I missed it when I took a look round earlier,' said Ryan. 'But I did find this. It may have nothing to do with the mystery woman, of course.' He took out his wallet and produced a tiny scrap of deep pink fabric.

'Let me see.' Susie peered at the fragment. 'I think that shade matches the jacket the woman was wearing. Mrs Ferguson's not a pink kind of person, so it can't be hers.'

'Ahem! Might I ask you all if there's any more evidence squirrelled away?' Greg peered over his specs.

'I didn't find anything else.' Hannah shook her head.

'Nor me,' said Ryan. 'Honest, guv. And, as I told Hannah, I couldn't find any significant footprints because of the weeds all over the ground.'

'Well, I think our friend here makes an excellent point,' said Greg. 'And I happen to know just the person to trust with the information we've obtained. Would you permit me to pursue a certain line of inquiry? Having you three young people on the case, spreading the word, makes the old saying that time is of the essence even more relevant than before.'

'Fine by me,' said Ryan.

'You guys are in charge,' said Jack. 'I'll help with the groundwork, like I said. So, are you making a move soon? I should get on.'

'Of course,' said Hannah. 'Time is money for you. It'll save you some time if you stop off at the shop and pick up some missing-dog leaflets when you're passing. It's very kind of you to offer to help, especially after we were so suspicious of you.'

Susie chipped in, 'Mr Russell, could you come back this afternoon when the vicar's here? He was muttering about the dripping tap in the bathroom, but I know he definitely wants help with the garden. If we're blessed with a fine day for the flower and produce show, we'll be serving teas outside, you see.'

'Of course I'll come back. Thank you. I've noticed there are plenty of great flowers, but, as Ryan pointed out, the weeds are running riot.'

'Can't see the wood for the trees,' said Greg. 'That's often the case in life.'

Hannah was holding the earring up and peering at it. 'Sorry to be a pain, but do you have a magnifying glass, Susie?'

'This is a vicarage, Hannah. We could probably kit out an expeditionary force if push came to shove. Excuse me a moment.'

She hurried out of the kitchen.

'There's one lady who seems more cheerful,' commented Greg.

'I think she's really grateful for our help,' said Hannah. 'You can imagine how distraught she was yesterday but let's not go there.'

'Quite. A positive attitude is vital,' said her grandfather.

Susie quickly returned, brandishing a large, black-handled magnifying glass. 'We keep this in the hall table drawer. The vicar, bless him, still uses an old telephone directory.'

'Thank you.' Hannah bent over the single earring while the men got to their feet and began thanking the house-keeper for her hospitality.

'Yes!' Hannah rose to her feet too.

'What have you spotted?' Ryan asked.

'An initial. The letter R is engraved in the little gold disc from which the dropper thing hangs.'

'I'm sure that's very interesting, but how many girls' names begin with an R?'

'Shedloads, I guess,' said Jack.

'Well, for a start, there's Rebecca, Rachel, Rosemary, Renee, Rita — '

'Um, yes, I know, Granddad,' said Hannah hastily. 'But R also happens to be the first letter of the central jewel. I know you'll probably all laugh at me, but I wouldn't mind betting the woman who owns this and who we think must've left through the window is called Ruby.'

'I've certainly never seen Mrs Ferguson wearing rubies; nor Jodie, for that matter,' said Susie.

'It'd be strange if either of them had lost an earring and not asked you to keep an eye out for it,' said Hannah. 'Anyway, Jodie hasn't been home since early June, has she?'

Susie shook her head.

Hannah watched the men's reactions. Jack also shook his head, but as if saying *Yeah, right, if you say so.* Ryan shot her a quizzical look as if he was sceptical but also willing to keep an open mind.

Her grandfather, however, nodded his head and beamed at her. 'Well, I'm blessed! You remind me of your grandmother and the way she used to have her hunches about this and that. So I wouldn't discount your theory, Hannah; and if you're happy to leave this matter with me, I'll see what I can establish.'

* * *

'I need to get out of the village for a day.' Ryan reached for Hannah's hand.

223

She glanced at his profile as they strolled away from the vicarage. 'That sounds a bit dramatic. Any special reason?'

'Inspiration. I want to visit a museum of some sort, maybe an art gallery but either will do. How about keeping me company?'

She squeezed his fingers. 'If you don't think I'll be in your way, yes, I'd love to come with you.'

'I wouldn't have invited you if I'd thought you'd be in my way. I need a change of scene but I also want to be with you somewhere we can enjoy each other's company without any thoughts of dogs or hungry customers or — or — '

'Jumping out of vicarage windows and worrying about missing pieces in jigsaw puzzles?'

'Exactly. I'm keen to help with all that but, like my mum says, a change is as good as a rest. All this forensic kind of thinking isn't helping my creativity.' His forehead creased. 'Sorry, I don't mean to sound selfish. Will Greg be okay without you around?'

Hannah chuckled. 'The Silver Surfers' Club meets tomorrow afternoon. He told me he's giving them a talk on search engines. In return, he gets a cream tea — and I wouldn't mind betting, an invitation to Sunday lunch from one of the widows that keep an eye on him.'

'Sounds like it's not a bad life for the old folk living here,' said Ryan. 'Not so sure about the teenagers.'

'I suppose they rely on their friends. I'm not sure what it's like for the pensioners who don't have family nearby. Mum orders Granddad's online big shop, and Dad usually drives him when he has an appointment at the optician's or needs a haircut.'

'He's one of the lucky ones.'

'Can you see yourself coming back here to live, after you get your degree?'

'No way,' said Ryan. 'How about you?'

'That would depend. If I can find a

teaching job within twenty miles of home, my folks will probably let me live with them so I can save money on rent.'

'And spend it on running a car.'

She groaned. 'I haven't even passed my test yet. Maybe I'd be better living in a city and sharing a flat.'

'Go back to London, maybe?'

Hannah hesitated. 'I do miss London, sometimes.'

'Only sometimes?'

'The part we lived in was great, and I was sorry in a way to leave. London's a brilliant place to be if you're into shops, different foods, sightseeing — '

'Culture?'

'Of course. I've seen loads of plays and films over the years, and I've been to the big museums with the school or with Mum and Dad. Somehow, I prefer visiting stately homes, and seeing furniture and paintings in the places the family put them.'

'I think I know where to take you tomorrow.'

'But tomorrow's for you, Ryan. I'm

just coming along for the ride.'

He stopped suddenly. Gently, he tipped her chin so her face tilted towards his as he kissed her. Hardly had their lips met when a loud squawking split the still air, a noise so raucous and intrusive that both Hannah and Ryan collapsed into spontaneous laughter.

'Talk about ruining a romantic moment!' Ryan pointed. 'Look at the little pest, flying round and showing off in front of his duck friends.'

Hannah gazed round. 'Never mind him. There's a gang of primary school children just walking down the road. Looks like the teachers are taking them on a walk.'

He grabbed her hand again. 'Let's go. In case they're doing a survey or something.'

She could hardly hurry for laughing. 'That'll be me, one day. Taking my class out of school and into the big world so they can see it through different eyes. I can't wait!'

All of a sudden he was serious again.

'No! Don't let's talk about the future. Not yet. Let's be young and silly just a bit longer. Please, Hannah.'

She felt a pang of sadness for him. He had massive talent and probably put up with a lot of pressure to do well on his course. But in many ways, she felt he'd needed to grow up sooner than she had.

'Okay. We'll concentrate on the moment. But for now, if you're not needed back at the pub, we really should get on with spreading the word about the second dog theft.'

'If I come back with you, you can give me my share of the flyers, plus some to leave at the shop so there's plenty for Jack to collect. He told me he's calling at the houses in Bailsford Bottom, so how about I take the school end as far as The Seven Stars?'

'Excellent. That leaves me to do Manor View and the old estate workers' cottages.'

'I'm working tonight but I'd like to pick you up at nine tomorrow morning ready for our day out. Is that okay?'

'Great. I'll keep an eye on what's happening online but mainly I'll be catching up on my reading tonight.'

*　*　*

Next day, she wondered if Ryan would drive them to Bath, maybe visit the Costume Museum or the American Museum at Claverton Down. But she soon realised they wouldn't be treading the same streets as Jane Austen had, which Hannah had read about in more than one classic novel.

She was thinking about ladies wearing bonnets, and wondering what it would have felt like to be paraded at social events and eyed up as a potential wife, while Ryan steered the car along a road Hannah felt must be in the middle of nowhere.

'What's so funny?'

'I'm not laughing!' She glanced sideways at him.

'Maybe not aloud,' he said.

'If you really want to know, I was thinking about Regency times, and what it would've been like to be a woman then.'

'Pretty boring, I imagine. You'd have had to learn to sew.'

She shuddered. 'I'd have been the studious one, nose in a book, while my sisters chattered about ribbons and lace and the next big ball and whether there'd be any handsome military men there. Gross.'

'I kind of wish we could go back in time, though. Like, hop in a TARDIS and set the co-ordinates for the early nineteenth century. I'd like that.'

'Is that why you're hoping to find inspiration today? So you can revisit history in your art — minus the time-travel?'

'Maybe. My paintings are becoming a bit countrified. Like I said, I need inspiration.'

'But, Ryan, with an imagination like yours, I wouldn't have thought that was a problem. Your pictures tell such a story. Not that I'm not pleased to be away from the village for a while.'

'I enjoy using my imagination so the duck pond becomes like a miniature harbour, of course I do.'

'Or the Mediterranean Ocean with cruise liners and millionaires' yachts sailing on it?'

'You like that one, don't you?'

'It's fantastic.'

'Thanks, but getting away from familiar places is good for my creativity.' He groaned. 'That didn't come out right. I don't mean to sound like I'm someone special.'

'But you are special, Ryan. You're not just a good artist, you can take an image and transform it into something out of this world.'

'I might quote that in my CV.'

'So where are we going? Do you have a TARDIS parked somewhere in the Cotswolds?'

'I wish! We'll be there soon so you haven't long to wait.'

Hannah looked at hedgerows, fields

with cattle grazing contentedly, and sturdy farmhouses. She peered down farm tracks as they passed by, some with notice boards advertising Bed and Breakfast or free-range eggs and organic vegetables for sale.

Ryan slowed the car, ready to drive through a pretty village. Hannah saw chocolate-box thatched cottages and white-painted fences, a grey stone church with a stream gently babbling nearby.

'This looks too good to be true,' she said. 'It's like Bailsford but much more posh. I wouldn't be surprised if it's been used in a television drama.'

'My mother told me two of the Royals live somewhere around here.'

'Did she say which?'

'Um, a duke and duchess?'

Hannah giggled. 'Typical bloke. I bet your mum remembers their names.'

'Okay, it's the Duke and Duchess of Trumpington.'

'I suppose I'd better not thump you while you're driving.'

'Not if you want to arrive in one piece.'

Hannah spotted a brown sign bearing the symbol of a manor house and the name of a well-known stately home. She glanced at her chauffeur again, but his face remained expressionless.

At the next turning, he steered the car down a leafy lane and drove over the cattle grid at the entrance to a big car park, pulling into a space near the ticket office.

'I was just hoping you were heading for Wellfield Manor. How lovely.' Impulsively, she leaned in and kissed Ryan's left cheek. 'You couldn't have chosen anywhere better.'

'Do you know much about it?'

'Only what my parents have said. They belong to the National Trust, so they like to go somewhere different every month. My mother thinks Wellfield's the best stately home they've visited so far.'

'Cool. Let's get going. There's quite a bit to see, so maybe we should look at a map.'

'That sounds too much like being

organised.' She stopped and grabbed his arm. 'Please let me buy our tickets. It's only fair.'

'My treat. This is our first proper date, isn't it?'

She felt a warm glow of pleasure. 'I suppose it is. Unless you count that lovely tea or hanging out amongst the tombstones.'

They walked in silence along the ruler-straight, tree-lined driveway. At the great house's front entrance, Hannah expected to have the contents of her handbag looked over; but the smiling woman, wearing a navy-blue jacket and skirt, simply checked their tickets and handed them each a leaflet.

'It's very peaceful. Very laid-back,' said Hannah as she and Ryan stood to one side and gazed at the map he'd unfolded.

'Well, you're in the sticks now. What do you fancy first?'

'I'd like to start with the servants' quarters. If you're researching, I'm going to do the same. I'd like to make notes so I can write the diary of one of the kitchen maids, with some photos or postcards.'

'Cool. I'm happy to start there too.' He stuffed the leaflet into his pocket.

They linked hands and headed for the door to the domestic quarters.

'I feel as if someone's dropped me inside Downton Abbey,' said Hannah. 'I'd probably have been more suitable as a kitchen maid than a lady's maid, though.'

Ryan made no comment. Hannah wondered if he'd even heard of the famous television series, but decided he must have though it probably wasn't his kind of thing. She noticed they were entering a very different world from the one glimpsed when they'd walked across the vast marble-floored entrance hall with sweeping staircase and ornate chandeliers glittering like something from a fairytale ballroom.

'Oh, wow,' said Hannah as they walked into the big kitchen and saw the still model figures of various domestic staff, positioned going about their duties. 'This looks so realistic.'

Other visitors were ahead of them. A woman and a little girl were studying the cook figure that wore a starched white apron and mobcap. The face was rosy, as if this kitchen queen had truly been bending over bubbling stews and opening oven doors to check on roasting meats.

'Is she real, Mummy?' Hannah heard the child's question and was suddenly reminded of her five-year-old self, on a visit to Madame Tussauds in London, when she'd come face to face with a policeman standing at the bottom of a flight of stairs and decided he must be real.

Ryan pointed to a table where two kitchen maid figures were mixing and rolling pastry. 'I'm going to take some photos,' he said. 'I can't see any notices forbidding it.'

Hannah wandered over to a pantry, its door open to display shelves lined with packets, bottles and jars. This was the kind of thing she was keen on including in her project. It might well be useful when that far-off day came that she'd be standing before a class of children and taking her first lesson.

But while she was lost in thought, Ryan was impatient to move on. 'You can come back later,' he said. 'I'm starving. Let's find the coffee shop.'

'When are you not starving?' She allowed herself to be drawn away. Already in her mind's eye she could picture children making drawings of platefuls of food and cutting them out. The life of a skivvy, a footman or a lad earning a pittance cleaning the family's boots and shoes and running errands — all these things beckoned.

'Thank you so much for bringing me,' she said. 'You're absolutely right. It's good to get away from Bailsford. I can see now, I was becoming a bit obsessed with you-know-what.'

He put his forefinger to his lips.

She nodded. 'Come on, then! Time

for tea and muffins, and this time it's my treat.'

⋆ ⋆ ⋆

Hannah decided to explore the grounds while Ryan took photographs of furniture he wanted to miniaturize. She approved of his decision to paint a picture of a dolls' house whirling through space.

The stately home's kitchen garden was still fully functioning, with a couple of workers bent over the vegetable beds. Hannah imagined that, had she been an Ivy or a Daisy back in the day, she would have been coming out here to pluck fresh herbs or summer fruits. She jotted down a few notes on her pad.

Still locked in another century, she walked around the side of the mansion and took a path leading past flowerbeds and through a small copse. She emerged at the top of a grassy slope. At the bottom lay a lake, shimmering in the sunshine. Waterfowl dotted the surface and a couple of ducks sat on the grass.

It was the perfect backdrop for her to let her imagination fly and mentally upgrade her social status. She could become, perhaps Lady Rose. Who might Ryan play in her romantic fantasy? She sat down on the grass and closed her eyes, enjoying the warm sunshine on her face and the soft breeze rippling her hair.

She didn't know how long she sat there but her imagination had been fired because she was back in time, drawing on a much earlier author's fiction, and fantasising about Mr Darcy wading from the lake, his drenched shirt clinging to his manly chest.

'Who are you dreaming of?'

Hannah opened her eyes. 'You don't want to know!'

Ryan pulled a face. 'You girlies!' He held out his hand.

She clutched it and got to her feet.

He pulled her to him. 'It's no fun on my own, so I came to find you.'

'You're supposed to be doing a work project, Ryan!'

'But I need a model. Are you up for it?'

'Will you make me into Lady Rose?'

'Sorry?'

Hannah giggled. 'Am I family or staff?'

'Both,' he said. 'You have that kind of face.'

12

Next morning, Hannah was munching toast and marmalade while trying to avoid showering crumbs on the book propped against her mum's pottery cruet. She was scheduled to work at the shop that afternoon, so didn't need to rush out early after the enjoyable outing of the day before.

Her phone buzzed as a text message homed in. She reached out and blinked as the words appeared on the screen.

Dog snatched from local beauty spot. Speak soon. At shop now.

Her granddad's newsflash wasn't welcome, but one thing was clear as the glass of cold water she was drinking. Bailsford's amateur detective team needed to get on the case and stop this horrible string of wrongdoings from becoming any longer.

Hannah decided to call on Greg as

241

soon as she'd finished breakfast. But she wouldn't yet alert Ryan, as he'd told her he planned to shut himself away and start sketching everything he could see in his mind. He must have taken dozens of photographs, many of her in various rooms. She'd enjoyed playing lady of the manor, but was even more thrilled when one of the staff took an interest in what they were doing and produced a maid's outfit used by actors for special promotions. So Hannah became a Daisy or an Ivy in sober grey frock and voluminous white apron, complete with hair tucked into a cap, as fitted her lowly status.

★ ★ ★

When she pushed open the door of the village stores, her granddad was helping an old lady pack her purchases into her shopping trolley. Hannah waited patiently while he chatted to the customer, and made sure she safely negotiated the shallow step down to street level, before greeting Greg.

'Where exactly did it happen?'

'Cleaver Lakes. Do you know where I mean?'

'Is it that wetlands area they started creating while we still lived in London?'

'That's the place. At least the local radio station has picked up on the fact that no less than three dogs have disappeared in a relatively short space of time.'

'I imagine this third one must've been off the lead when it got taken?'

'Presumably. It might have strayed into the woodland bit to check out exciting smells, and maybe the owner hadn't even started calling it when someone grabbed it.'

Hannah sighed. 'People are so trusting. Who wouldn't want to give their pet a chance to roam around somewhere away from traffic? But you wouldn't let a small child wander off on its own, would you?'

'Indeed you would not. I'm not sure how the animal could have been taken away so smartly, though. Unless it strayed close to the car park and someone took a fancy to it.'

'It could be that the thief used something to lure the dog. Some titbit containing a drug, maybe.' Hannah screwed up her face. 'It's such a sickening thought, Granddad. But I'm beginning to think like a criminal, aren't I?'

He nodded. 'In cases like these, I think one has to. The police don't have the resources to devote the kind of time we're spending on this. If only we could establish even one similarity, that would point us in the right direction. That might indicate that these thefts are all down to the same person.'

'We don't even know if that person has an accomplice. Dare I ask if you've had a chance to ask questions about the woman we think must've dropped that earring?'

'Not yet. Between you and me, I want to speak to Debbie and she's not here until later. Unfortunately, she wasn't on the roster for yesterday.'

'I doubt any of us could have pre-
vented that third theft from happening,
so don't beat yourself up, Granddad.'

He rubbed his chin. 'No, we must
remain positive. I have a hunch that this
spate of thefts is down to the same
person or persons. But I haven't asked
how you enjoyed your day out. Did
your knight in shining armour take you
somewhere exciting?' He shot her a sly
look. 'I suppose anywhere would be
exciting when you're with the one you
love.'

Hannah noticed a faraway look in his
eyes. She didn't want him to feel sad,
but she didn't want to seem unsympa-
thetic.

'We had a great time, thanks, if you
really want to know. Ryan took me to
Wellfield.'

'To the Manor? My goodness, that
young man of yours is full of surprises.
How very civilised of him.' He smiled
wistfully. 'Your grandmother used to
like me to take her there every year,

when the rhododendrons were in bloom.' He took out a large blue handkerchief and blew his nose. 'Memories, eh?'

★   ★   ★

That afternoon, while Debbie was in the stockroom, Hannah occupied herself by tidying the bottom shelves of the toiletries section. Chaos had arrived in the form of a high-spirited toddler, who took advantage of Hannah and his mum discussing a newspaper headline about the engagement of two sporting celebrities. Tubes of toothpaste and bars of soap were obviously far more interesting than the toy car the little boy had been clutching when his mum brought him into the shop.

'Hi, Hannah.'

The voice was male. She scrambled to her feet and rounded the big chill cabinet to check out its owner.

'Hey, Jack, I almost didn't recognise you.'

Jack Russell shuffled his feet. 'Yeah, well, being taken for a robber rattled my cage, to be honest. It had much more effect on me than my mum's nagging!' He grinned at Hannah. 'Hopefully I look less of a hooligan now I've shaved and had my hair cut.'

'I feel awful now, jumping to conclusions like I did. Especially as you were with Ben when I first saw you. Ryan and I couldn't figure out what you were doing driving down Manor View if you were on your way back to Bristol.'

'Ben and I met at college, and we get together now and then. Sometimes I fancy the bright lights, and he lets me crash at his place. We went clubbing on the Saturday night, and he remembered his folks were expecting him for Sunday lunch, so I drove him back to Bailsford — and ended up eating with them too, of course.'

'Round here, Sunday buses are like gold dust,' said Hannah.

'So I gather. Anyway, talking to Ben's

father, I discovered a gap in the market, so to speak. Ben showed me round areas of the village where he thought I might pick up some repair jobs before I took him back. When we drove down your road, he spotted you, so I pulled up.'

'You did look a bit suss, you know. Keeping your head down as if you had something to hide.'

Jack swallowed hard. 'Yeah, I know. I was gobsmacked, to be honest. Seeing you, and realising a girl like you would never give me a second glance. And Ben was talking enough for three, wasn't he? I couldn't figure out if the guy with you was a serious boyfriend or just a mate, but I guess that's what Ryan is. Serious, I mean. So I s'pose it's pointless asking you to go out some time?'

Hannah stared back at him. She hadn't seen that coming. The door flew open to admit a small group of primary school children. They shrugged off their backpacks and placed them neatly beside the counter.

'Hi, girls,' said Hannah. 'Just off the school bus?'

But they were already heading, chattering like magpies, for the magazine rack. Hannah didn't know quite where to look. Didn't quite know what to say to this young man.

Her phone buzzed.

'It's okay — I just want a box of chocolates,' said Jack. 'You sort out your message.'

He headed across to the confectionery display to examine the shelves. Probably, thought Hannah, he wanted to buy his mum a treat. 'If it's for a gift, those ones in the red box are fantastic,' she said. 'You get a selection of white, dark and milk chocolate all in together.'

'Cheers,' said Jack.

She checked her text. It was from Ryan. *How about a game of tennis 2nite?*

She decided not to answer it straight away, and slipped her phone back in her pocket. A glance at Jack told her he was dawdling, maybe waiting for the school-girls to leave. They didn't hang about, paying for their sweets and comics and calling goodbyes as they collected their backpacks and, still giggling and chatting, set the doorbell clanging on their way out.

Jack walked towards her. 'It's okay, Hannah. I'm not trying to make life difficult for you. It's only that Ben said something about Ryan going out with the vicar's daughter — Jodie, is it? That kind of set me wondering if you and he really were just mates and nothing else.'

'It's, um, complicated. I've got a lot on my mind just now.'

He smiled at her, his eyes kind. 'I'm not going anywhere,' he said. 'I mean, I'll be in and out of the village now I've picked up some good Bailsford customers.' He placed the pack of chocolates on the counter and held out a ten-pound note.

'Would you like a bag?'

'No, thanks.'

She counted his change into his palm.

He picked up the package of chocolates and held it out to her. 'These are for you, Hannah. And, by the way, my visits to so many different houses have made me think much more about security measures. Some people are amazingly trusting, like they're living back in the 1940s or something. Others go in for security alarms and CCTV cameras.'

'It's the kind of thing I haven't thought about. I imagine Mr and Mrs Andrews won't ever forget how they used to leave that back door unlocked.' She looked down at the gift he'd given her. 'Jack, this is very kind of you, but I mustn't let you spend your money on chocolates for me. Goodness, I hope Granddad didn't drop hints about it being my birthday soon?'

'No way. So when's your birthday?'

'Um, in a while.'

'Is it your eighteenth?'

'Come on! My twentieth, if you don't mind!'

He grinned. 'Well, enjoy the chocolates anyway. You've been very kind to me, and not just by making me improve my image.' He moved towards the door. 'I almost forgot. You might like to consider something I noticed near the gateway to the big, posh house opposite the vicarage.'

'Oh, what's that, then?'

'Let's just say those people are very security-conscious. With the CCTV camera angled the way it is, I think your female dog thief could well have been filmed if she had a car parked alongside the vicarage wall. I'd say it's definitely worth calling on the owners of that house and having a word.'

'I don't know the people, but I expect my granddad does.'

'You might like to take this opportunity to meet them. I think they're a nice couple.' He winked at her. 'Especially as they've asked me to keep their swimming pool clean over the rest of the summer, plus their front and back lawns. Go for it, Hannah. What have you got to lose?'

'You're right. We daren't risk missing what might be vital evidence.'

'Good for you. Now, I'd better push off.' He opened the door but turned his head towards Hannah. 'Maybe I spoke out of turn when I made that comment about Ryan and Jodie. If so, I apologise.'

He shot out of the shop, closing the door quietly behind him, leaving Hannah staring at the space where he'd been standing.

* * *

Debbie emerged from the stockroom not long after Jack Russell left.

'Hannah, why don't you knock off now? I've finished what I needed to do so I can stay put. Greg's calling to see me about some urgent matter, so if we do get a rush, he'll help out.'

'If you're sure, that'd be very helpful. I need to call on someone as soon as possible.'

'My goodness, do you ever sit still?'

'Sometimes!'

'Well, Greg sounded very mysterious on the phone and you're always so busy, Hannah.'

'I've got pretty involved in this dog theft stuff, Debbie.'

Both turned towards the door as the bell clanged and Greg walked in.

'Granddad, we should meet up later. You've got stuff to discuss with Debbie and I've just been given a tip off so I need to follow it up before I go home.' Hannah frowned. 'Oh, and Ryan wants me to play tennis later and I really could do with the exercise.'

'You should give him a game, then. Plenty of time to meet up afterwards — in fact, we could all have a drink in The Seven Stars' beer garden.'

'Any excuse.' Debbie chortled, hands on hips. 'Honestly, listening to you two really does make me feel I'm in a TV cosy crime series.'

'I believe we'd make an unlikely pairing of detectives, Debbie. Though I always did fancy myself as John Steed.' Greg smiled. 'How about seven-thirty in the beer garden, Hannah?'

'Perfect.' Hannah headed into the back to collect her shoulder bag.

Greg looked at Debbie. 'I need to ask some questions, and something tells me you're the best person to answer them.'

★　★　★

At six o'clock, Hannah met Ryan at the recreation ground. He wore his khaki cut-offs, a black T-shirt, and important-looking trainers. On his head, he'd tied a bandanna.

'You look worryingly keen.' Hannah grinned at him. 'I hope I shan't regret agreeing to play tennis with you.'

'No worries. I'm out of practice.'

'That makes two of us.'

'I suppose you used to play tennis with Jodie.' Hannah held her breath as they walked towards the court and Ryan took out his key to unfasten the padlock. Was it her imagination, or was he taking a long time to answer?

'Um, here we go, then,' he said. 'There's another booking at seven, so we better crack on. I'll go down the other end and we'll knock up, okay?'

He obviously didn't want to give anything away. But then, she hadn't mentioned her visit to Mulberry House, the beautiful property opposite the vicarage. She was determined to keep secret what she'd learned from the house owner until the meeting later, when she, Ryan and Greg would discuss their next move. Hopefully her grandfather's meeting with Debbie would have had a successful outcome, but Hannah wasn't sure exactly what angle he was pursuing.

She picked up a ball and whacked it across the net. It bounced high, and Ryan swiped at it, but sent it spinning sideways.

'Hey, I didn't think I was taking on Serena Williams!'

'Sorry, I was thinking of something else. You give it a go.'

They started to hit, and Hannah began enjoying being back on a tennis court.

'You should do a coaching course,' said Ryan at last. 'It'll probably be very useful when you're teaching.'

'I thought you wanted to act like we're irresponsible kids.' She lobbed a ball way over his head, but he ran round it and whacked it back.

'Phew, I need to take a break if you're starting to play like Andy Murray.'

'I wish! Let's get a drink, then. I brought some water.'

They flopped down on the bench beside the court.

'Are you going to tell me why you look like you're bursting to tell me a secret?' He handed her a plastic bottle.

'Cheers. No, not 'til later when we have our strategy meeting.'

He muttered something.

'So, are you going to tell me whether you're missing Jodie? You do remember Jodie, I take it?'

He glugged water and screwed the

top back on his bottle. 'What is it with girls? Jodie and me, we're no longer an item. I'm not sure we ever were. Has someone been stirring things?'

She hesitated.

'I knew it! Is it Ben, by any chance? Has he been back since that time we saw him in Jack Russell's car?'

'Not to my knowledge.'

'Ah, I get it. It's Jack, isn't it? I could see the way he was looking at you when we were all in the vicarage kitchen. Has he asked you out?'

'I don't see what that has to do with you, Ryan.' Hannah hoped her cheeks were already so pink from running around that they couldn't possibly become even more so.

'Yet you seem to feel entitled to question me about Jodie. I give up.' He jumped to his feet. 'Shall we call it a day here?'

'Flipping heck, you're touchy.'

Suddenly he threw his tennis racquet down on the court so it bounced. He turned to her, eyes blazing.

Hannah met his gaze. She didn't flinch, didn't make a sarcastic comment, but stood waiting to see what he did next.

He put his arms around her. 'I'm sorry, Hannah. I shouldn't have thrown my toys out of the pram, and I truly didn't mean to upset you.'

Relieved, she put her arms around him. 'Ew, I must be horribly sweaty! I'm sorry too, Ryan. It's just that there's so much going on with all the dog stuff. I had such a fabulous day out with you yesterday. But sometimes you treat me like a mate, and sometimes like I'm your girlfriend. It's difficult to know how to react.'

He kissed the tip of her nose. 'I thought I'd found a new friend, but now I know different.'

She stiffened. *What now?*

He held her at arms' length.

'I love you, Hannah. That's one very big reason why I want to capture you in my paintings. Does that answer your question?'

Not even annoying comments and whistles from a group of village lads kicking a football around could interfere with Ryan and Hannah's tender kiss.

13

Hannah wondered how her grandfather might react when she and Ryan strolled hand-in-hand into the inn's garden and made their way to his table. But he must have become used to them, as he merely beamed and gave them a wave.

'I've left cash behind the bar with your dad, Ryan. Maybe you wouldn't mind fetching some drinks? I'll have another half of cider, please.'

'Cool. Thanks, Greg.' Ryan sped away, with one backward glance at Hannah.

She sat down opposite Greg. 'Are you okay, Granddad? You look a bit tired.'

'I could do with a good night's sleep,' he said. 'Old brain was working overtime last night, but now I'm feeling rather pleased with myself.'

'That makes two of us,' she said.

Greg inclined his head towards the inn. 'That wouldn't have anything to do with Mr Wonderful, I suppose?'

'That'd be telling! No, I've discovered something interesting — but my informant was Jack Russell, not Ryan.'

'Ah, so the plot thickens.' He pulled out a notebook and pencil. 'We need to make a list.'

Hannah chuckled. 'Another list?'

'This time, hopefully we're a lot closer to solving this mystery than we ever were before.'

Hannah nodded. The evening sunshine threw long shadows on the grass and several people had settled around the tables, enjoying a drink in peace. The rear of the inn faced on to a quiet road; with the birdsong, London seemed a very long way away.

Ryan returned, carrying a tray. He placed Hannah's glass of cider before her, and replaced Greg's empty glass with a full one.

'Cheers,' he said. 'Here's to the pursuit of crime!'

'That could be taken the wrong way,' said Greg.

'Maybe I mean the pursuit of criminals.' Ryan sat down next to Hannah. 'Sadly, I have nothing to contribute except for one piece of information I heard at lunchtime today, in the bar.'

Greg held up a hand. 'We should each take turns to relay information, don't you think?'

'Mine isn't concrete,' said Hannah. 'But it could be very important.'

'Right. How about you go first?' said Greg.

Ryan nodded.

Hannah took a deep breath. 'Jack Russell came into the shop today and told me something very interesting. He's been working for the people at Mulberry House, and noticed they have a security camera positioned in such a way that it's possible Susie's visitor has been captured on film. I have permission to go back tomorrow when Mr Carter's at home. Apparently he's the only one who understands the system.'

'Wow,' said Ryan. 'What a coup that'd be.'

'Yes, indeed,' said Greg.

'I'd prefer one of you to come with me.' Hannah looked from one to the other of them. 'Two heads are better than one.'

'How about you, Ryan? Your eyesight's better than mine.'

'Fine by me, but isn't Susie the one who should be there?'

'Good point,' said Hannah. 'I'll ring her first thing tomorrow.'

'Okay. Now, shall I tell you what I heard earlier? It may not mean anything, of course.'

'Let's hear it, then.' Greg folded his arms in front of him.

'According to a guy who lives near Cleaver Lakes, there's a couple who are renting a holiday cottage in his neck of the woods. By the way, this guy is a twitcher.'

'A what?' Hannah asked.

'A birdwatcher, darling,' said Greg.

'Anyway,' said Ryan. 'He was going

on about how he walked past this holiday cottage while a couple were unloading stuff from their car. It seemed to be just a couple of suitcases and some supermarket plastic bags — indicating, he thought, that the two of them must be on their own. He called good morning, but they either didn't hear or chose not to.

'He took that same way home afterwards, and all was quiet. Next day he went back to check on a bird he was keen on spotting, and he heard the sound of barking coming from inside the cottage.'

'I think I know where this is going. Being a twitcher and used to observing, this man thought it was strange that he hadn't seen a dog basket and any other canine paraphernalia being unloaded the day before?'

'Exactly, Greg. And he met the woman on one of the pathways when he was going home for lunch, so he greeted her and asked how they were settling in.'

'Persistent blighter, isn't he? Just the

kind of chap we need,' said Greg.

'Well, he assumed this person would be walking a dog, having heard one barking, but she definitely wasn't. That made him puzzled when he went past the place a couple of days later — on that occasion, he thought he could hear two different barks from inside. One sounded deep, and the other he described as more like yelping.'

Hannah leaned forward. 'Like a puppy? Stop keeping us in suspense!'

Ryan grinned. 'The guy saw the car was missing, so took a chance and walked up the path to take a look through the windows. He admits he shouldn't have, but on first sight, he just didn't like the look of the man. Said he looked shifty.'

'What did our twitcher friend see?'

'All the blinds or curtains were closed, Greg. But round the back of the cottage he could hear barking coming from inside. The window was open and he was convinced there must be two dogs in the room.'

'It's not much to go on, but I agree it's strange,' said Greg.

'If you rented a holiday cottage, why would you suddenly acquire a dog — then a second one — and leave them on their own while you went out?' Hannah wrung her hands. 'It sounds iffy to me. Did he say what the car was like?'

'My father asked him, and he described it as a very ordinary black saloon. Dad said maybe he should take a note of the number plate if he happened to see the vehicle again. That's all, really.' Ryan took a swallow of lager.

'That's significant, I'd say. Your turn now, Granddad.'

Greg nodded. He took the small box containing the ruby earring from his inside pocket and placed it on the table.

'I took this to the shop earlier and showed it to Debbie. Her reaction was immediate. Apparently she's received a phone call from a woman saying she'd visited Bailsford recently, tracking down ancient forebears in the churchyard.'

'Oh, please, not another ghoul!'

'Shush, Hannah,' said Ryan. 'A lady at the table over there looks really worried.'

'Shall I go on?'

'Please, Greg,' said Ryan.

'The gist of it is, the woman said she'd lost a very valuable earring while visiting, and she'd be grateful if Debbie could let her know if someone found it and brought it into the shop. Obviously she knew there was no local police station.'

'Hey, did she leave her name? A contact number?' Ryan sat forward, his eyes fixed on Greg.

'She'd leave a false one, Ryan. I bet Sheila McCarthy's not the woman's real name either,' said Hannah.

'Whoever she is told Debbie her name was Liz. She also said she was planning to leave the area very soon, but was prepared to offer a small reward for return of her jewellery.'

'I bet she was,' muttered Hannah.

'Did Debbie give you the number?' Ryan asked.

'Of course. She enquired whether the woman did in fact visit the shop while she was in Bailsford, but either she truly hadn't or else she was telling a porky pie.'

'No surprise there,' said Hannah. 'We need to move fast, but we can't check out that camera until tomorrow. If it comes up with a shot of a black car parked outside the vicarage — '

'And if our mystery woman's caught on it, then Debbie can take a look at the image and tell us if that's Mrs Sheila McCarthy. Hoorah!'

Hannah watched her grandfather's face light up. He looked much more cheerful than he had when they first arrived.

'You really, really care about these pets, don't you?' She spoke softly.

'I do, darling. I hate the thought of needless suffering brought about through people's greed. And the sooner we can reunite those dogs with their poor bereft owners, the better it'll be.'

'Can't we just turn up at that holiday cottage and confront her?' Ryan asked. 'You'd recognise the first two dogs, Greg, wouldn't you?'

'Oh, I think so, my boy. But my gut feeling is, if we can produce that evidence on film and hand it over to the police, they'll move in fast, and they have far more clout than we do.'

'I'd feel happier if we knew the car registration number.' Ryan's face set in a grim expression.

'Don't forget, we have something the woman is very keen to recover,' said Greg.

'Of course! How about if one of us rings to tell her we've found her earring, and asks what we should do next?' Hannah felt a surge of excitement.

'Better still, ask Debbie to do that tomorrow,' said Ryan. 'Meantime, I can ask Dad to get his twitcher customer to check out the happy holidaymakers. If we're on the right track, there should be three different kinds of woofing coming from the house.'

'If it's the area I'm thinking of, there aren't many other dwellings near that cottage. It's the perfect hideaway, especially for someone hoping to keep a low profile.' Greg looked at Ryan. 'Maybe we should back off at this stage. I wouldn't want the friendly twitcher to put himself at risk.'

'Surely that wouldn't happen?' Hannah raised her eyebrows, but her grandfather didn't say a word.

14

Next morning, a tall man opened the door of Mulberry House to Hannah and Susie, a mobile phone clamped to one ear. Hannah thought he looked just as she imagined a high-flying business-man to be. He beckoned them inside.

'Cheers, Charles,' he said. 'I'll call you back in a bit after I've made my decision.' He closed the call and surveyed his visitors. 'Good morning — so sorry about that. Now, let's get this show on the road for you. I have to make some more calls, so I'll be in the next room if you need me.' He looked at Hannah. 'I'd better make sure you understand how to pause the footage. Is that all right?'

'It is. Thanks, Mr Carter.'

'I only hope it'll do some good. Wretched people, hope they get pros-ecuted.'

'Our main concern is the animals; but yes, it's all very distressing.'

Mr Carter peered at Susie. 'I'm sorry, but don't I know you from somewhere?'

'I'm the housekeeper across the way; or the Girl Friday, as Mrs Ferguson calls me.'

'Ah, yes, I thought you looked familiar. Well, here we go, then. If you do find incriminating evidence, I've no objection to your calling the police so they can come and take a look.'

When they were left alone, Hannah patted Susie's hand. 'Don't be afraid to shout out if you spot something. I can note down the time it occurred to make it easier to find later. You're the only one of us who knows what Mrs Sheila McCarthy looks like, so I'm crossing fingers and toes!'

'Could we fast-forward, maybe, to save time? We're still at eight o'clock here.'

'Well spotted, Susie.' Hannah did what was necessary. 'I'll start it again at a quarter to ten, because I assume they wouldn't have wanted to be hanging around too long.'

Neither spoke a word — until both spotted a black saloon appear on the screen and park outside the vicarage.

'Bingo. Oh, I so wish we had that car number.' Hannah peered at the scene. 'I just can't make it out.'

'Pause it, please, Hannah. I just happen to have that magnifying glass with me.'

'You must've been a Girl Guide.' Hannah paused the film and waited.

'Yes! Write this down, please, Hannah. And if you start the film again, the footage should show a good view of Mrs McCarthy getting out of the car — and, hopefully, returning with little Juliet smuggled under her jacket.'

*   *   *

After the police logged what the three sleuths had discovered and assured them they'd be acting on the valuable information provided, Hannah felt a bit deflated. She couldn't wait to hear the missing pets were back with their respective owners. Of course, she was obliged not to say anything to anyone until the police took action and released an official statement.

Ryan had shut himself up in his room again, trying to finish a painting to be auctioned at the forthcoming flower and produce show. Hannah took her turn at the stores later, having to endure Debbie nagging her to enter something for the home produce section.

'I'm only a novice baker,' she said.

'It's a good cause; and the more baking you do, the better you'll get,' replied Debbie.

Hannah watched her dive below the counter and produce a pile of leaflets.

'These leftover show schedules may as well go on the counter, just in case someone wants to enter at the last minute.'

'I'd forgotten about it, with all that's

been going on,' said Hannah. 'Grand-dad used to be involved, but he's cut down his activities a bit.'

Debbie smiled. 'Not so as you'd notice. I meant to ask you, any news since your granddad asked about that woman who lost the earring?'

'Um, I'm not sure yet. I mean, maybe.'

'It's all right, Hannah. I did say that being around you and Greg was like hanging out with two amateur sleuths.' She hesitated. 'This may mean nothing, but I think I should tell you: I've had something niggling at me.'

Hannah waited.

'There was a girl in my class at school called Ruby. She moved away a couple of years after we all went up to the high school. When I spoke to that woman who called herself Liz, it didn't occur to me. But ever since you brought that earring in and said something about the owner's name maybe beginning with an R, I've been thinking about that phone call and how high-pitched the voice was. Just like I remember Ruby's.'

Hannah tried not to show her excitement. She needed to pass these details to the police. If the woman they suspected still had local connections, it might explain lots of things.

'Do you mind if I relay this to the police?'

'You do what you have to, my lovely.'

'It'd be a relief not having to worry all the time.'

'You're a good soul, Hannah. But you deserve some fun too.' She gave Hannah a mischievous look. 'I hear on the grapevine you and Ryan Hawkins are an item.'

'We're almost the same age. We hang out together. What possible interest could that be to anyone?'

Debbie threw her hands up in the air. 'Whoa, keep your hair on, young lady. People are pleased for you, I think. That boy's always been a bit of a loner. He's much more chatty with me when he pops in here now. I put that down to your influence.'

Hannah knew her cheeks were turning pink. 'I wouldn't know about that.'

To her relief she was saved from further interrogation when Jack Russell, wearing navy blue dungarees over a white T-shirt, entered the shop.

'Good morning, ladies,' he said, heading for the chill cabinet. 'Hi Hannah.' He treated her to a very lingering look.

Hannah realised her cheeks must now be turning a slightly paler shade of fuchsia; and to make matters worse, she saw that Debbie could hardly contain her curiosity.

'What was that about?' she hissed at Hannah through the corner of her mouth. 'How many boyfriends are you stringing along?'

'Look, Jack's just a friend.'

'If you say so. A friend who looks at you with big puppy-dog eyes.'

'Don't exaggerate, Debbie. Now shush, he's coming back.' It was

278

Hannah's turn to hiss.

'Are you coming to see the fun tomorrow, Mr Russell?' Debbie treated Jack to a big, bright smile.

'Sorry?'

'Debbie means the flower and produce show, Jack. It's an annual village affair,' said Hannah, wishing her cheeks would cool.

'Will there be food tasting?'

'I don't know.'

'There'll be food for sale, that's for sure,' said Debbie. 'You should enter for the Men's Big Bake Off.'

'I don't think so.' Jack placed his purchases on the counter.

'It's only for six fruit scones,' said Hannah. 'My granddad usually enters.'

'I might come along and hand out my flyers. Do you get a good crowd?'

'A very good crowd,' said Debbie. 'Mostly loyal followers who support it every year. Sometimes people's offspring visit for the weekend, so that's always nice. But I don't see why you shouldn't bring your flyers along.'

'You should make a poster,' said Hannah. 'I'm sure they'd let you stick it up somewhere. You might even take some bookings. Lots of people aren't around during the week, so it's a good chance to show your face.'

Debbie cleared her throat. 'Your turn to make the tea, Hannah. And Jack, if you like, I'll mention to the vicar's wife that you'd like to turn up tomorrow.'

'That would be amazing. Many thanks.' Jack grabbed his carrier bag. 'I must get going. Maybe see you ladies tomorrow, then. Thanks again for the advice.'

Debbie stared after him. 'Ooh, he's a bit like that actor who played Poldark, don't you think?'

Hannah shouted with laughter. 'I'll say one thing for you, Debbie, you certainly do cheer a person up.'

★ ★ ★

Hannah peered at rain-drenched foliage through the kitchen window. 'Well,

280

that'll save me a job tonight,' she muttered. If only her tummy would settle. She couldn't stop thinking about little Juliet and Toffee, not to mention the nameless pet snatched so recently. Even waking up to remember today was her twentieth birthday hadn't filled her with enthusiasm. Her parents had rung her last night, and her dad had said he'd transferred some money to her account.

Doubtless there would be birthday messages on her Facebook page. Her closest friends and family had sent cards, but she'd kept a low profile with her newest friends. It seemed heartless to expect a birthday celebration when those poor little dogs might be shivering, cold and lonely in some godforsaken hideaway.

But the police had their procedures, and no way could she ring up and waste their time asking questions that probably wouldn't be answered. Protocol was protocol, and she needed to be patient. She and her little team had done as much as they could.

The three layers of chocolate sandwich cake she'd baked the evening before stood under a plastic cover in the fridge. The filling — cream, melted dark chocolate and orange zest — was mixed, and waiting for her to spread it upon the cake layers, including the top. Hannah's final touch would be slivers of dark, white and milk chocolate.

A glance at the kitchen clock told her she'd plenty of time to get down to the village hall before the eleven o'clock deadline. But when the phone in the hall rang, she hoped whoever it was wouldn't stay on the line too long. Hannah crossed her fingers that it wasn't her grandfather in a tizzy over his scone dough.

She picked up the phone. 'Hannah speaking.'

At first, she thought she was hearing things. Wondered wildly if this was Ryan playing a trick on her — or maybe Jack. But they wouldn't do that to her, would they?

'I'm sorry. Could you say who you are again, please?'

'Sergeant Gibbs here, Miss Ross. We thought you'd like to know that all three missing dogs have now been restored to their owners. I think you'll be receiving a letter in due course, thanking you for all your efforts and for your community spirit.'

'Oh, my goodness. So you caught the thieves?'

Sergeant Gibbs coughed down the line. 'I'm not at liberty to release precise information on that score, Miss Ross. But a full statement will be issued to the press very soon.'

'Thank you, Sergeant.'

'Enjoy your day.'

The line went dead. Hannah put down the phone and jigged around the hallway. 'Yippee!' she yelled, before running into the kitchen to send a text to Ryan. Next, she picked up the hall phone again to call Greg. Even the weather seemed to have picked up on the happy news, and Hannah watched a beam of sunlight filter into the hallway.

★ ★ ★

She knocked on Mr and Mrs Andrews' front door as soon as she'd delivered her cake and entry form to the village hall.

'Oh, Hannah.' Mrs Andrews put her arms around her visitor. 'I can't thank you enough for all you've done to help us get Toffee back.'

'It was a combined operation,' said Hannah. 'I just had to come and tell you how thrilled I am.'

'My husband and the boy from next door have taken her to the recreation ground. She's had a full check-over by the police vet, but Mr Andrews thought she deserved a wee treat.'

'It's wonderful news. Maybe see you later at the show?'

'Definitely. We'll be bringing Toffee with us, of course, so she can thank you in person.'

Hannah had already spoken on the

phone to Susie, who'd received a joyful phone call from Mrs Ferguson. The vicar's wife, said Susie, was especially happy, as her daughter had managed to get home in time to join in the afternoon's fun at the flower and produce show.

Hannah hadn't spoken to Ryan. His mother, answering the phone at the pub after Hannah had decided he must have left his mobile somewhere inaccessible, sounded very mysterious. She said he had his hands full, but would see Hannah down at the duck pond just before two o'clock, when the editor of the local newspaper would declare the flower and produce show open.

Hannah — who was, to her dismay and puzzlement, unable to eat any lunch — changed into a pretty sundress in crisp white cotton, its fabric sprinkled with clusters of crimson cherries and tiny green leaves. The sun appeared to have forgotten how to creep behind the clouds, and as Hannah walked out of Manor View towards the centre of the village, she heard the sound of Bailsford's answer to Wet Wet Wet performing 'Love is All Around'.

Her heart performed a double bump as she saw Ryan walking towards her: looking, she decided, like the cat who'd eaten not only the cream, but a family fish supper into the bargain.

She couldn't stop smiling. To heck with appearing cool, because no way could she possibly remain unmoved, not when she could see him looking as if all his dreams were coming true. He didn't even bother to check who might be watching when he took her in his arms.

She nestled against him. 'Did your mum tell you the good news?'

'Yeah, it's amazing. Well done, Hannah. You and Greg both.'

'But you're part of it too, Ryan. You picked up on what that twitcher was saying in the bar. And we mustn't forget Jack. His tip-off was the clincher.'

'Yeah, Susie picking up the car

registration and being able to identify the woman made the police sit up and take notice of that CCTV footage. My dad's twitcher customer was asked to pick out the woman he'd seen from a gallery of photos.'

'I handed in the earring and the scrap of fabric but I guess they had what they wanted,' said Hannah. 'Granddad said Ruby had hoisted herself with her own petard. Debbie will be sad when she knows someone from her schooldays was involved.'

Ryan put his arm around her waist and they began walking towards the green. 'I'm sorry I didn't call you earlier, but I was trying to finish something.'

'You've entered the Men's Big Bake Off?'

'No way! I've been working on something entirely different.'

'Like?'

'Wait and see.'

'Ryan Hawkins, you can be so annoying, you know that?'

'Not half as annoying as you, Hannah Ross. Why didn't you tell me today was your birthday?'

'I didn't feel in a birthday mood. How did you find out, anyway?'

'Duh! How do you think?'

She knew it couldn't be Facebook. 'I'll give Granddad a talking-to when I see him.'

Ryan pulled a white envelope from inside his denim jacket. 'This is for you.'

She opened it carefully and took out a handmade card. 'It's beautiful. How long did that take you?'

'It's okay. I didn't really need to sleep last night.'

She looked closer at the watercolour scene he'd created. 'I'm in this! You've given the mermaid my face. Oh, Ryan. I'll treasure it for ever.'

He looked embarrassed. 'It's just a tryout. I'll give you your proper gift tomorrow.'

'I don't know what to say, except thank you.'

'You haven't seen my gift yet.'

She laughed at him. He reached out for a strand of her hair and drew it beneath her nose so she knew she looked like she'd grown a moustache. The pair of them wandered along, chattering, arms around each other, until they reached the green and Hannah heard someone call Ryan's name.

It was as if the magic spell was broken. Hannah turned; and there walking towards them was Jodie, looking, to her dismay, slimmer and fitter and more tanned, with her hair a brighter streaky-blonde than she'd ever seen it before.

'Hi Ryan. And Hannah Ross! Mum told me your folks had bought a house in the village.'

To Hannah's relief, Ryan not only kept his arm around her, but also squeezed her even closer.

'Dad told me what a help you've been over those awful dog thefts,' said Jodie. 'Thank you, Hannah.'

'I had plenty of support. I'm very relieved everything turned out well in the end.'

'Those puppies are so cute.' But her voice faded and her gaze focused in a different direction. 'Wow,' she said. 'Speaking about cute, how long has he been around? Does either of you have any idea who that guy is?'

Hannah turned to check. But Ryan was faster, and it was he who called to the young man the vicar's daughter had spotted.

'Hey, Jack. Come and join us. I don't think you've met Jodie, have you?'

* * *

Hannah's day kept on getting better and better. Granddad was awarded a Highly Commended for his scones, and decided that next year he'd aim for a top-three placing.

Ryan's mum won first prize for her beautiful cappuccino sponge layer cake. Mr Carter paid an astronomical sum of money for it, as he was vying with his own wife for the pleasure of adding to the church roof fund! Mr Andrews bid for Hannah's chocolate cake, which achieved third prize, and, after he bought it, invited she and Ryan to come round to tea next day so they could sample it.

Jodie, Hannah decided, was definitely less bossy than she remembered. Wandering around in a foursome, trying their hands at the game stalls and tucking into a delicious afternoon tea served by Debbie, Susie and helpers on the vicarage lawn, she felt she'd made another friend.

Ryan surprised her while they sat, watching children weaving amongst the tables, and chatting about their travels, their hopes and dreams.

He leaned towards her while Jodie and Jack were in deep conversation. 'I've decided it's time to grow up.'

'What's brought that on?'

'I don't want to lose you, Hannah. I don't want you to think of me as just the boy from the pub, someone to hang out with in the hols.'

'Who said I thought any such thing? And what makes you think I want to lose you?'

They gazed at each other.

'I've painted you a picture for your birthday. I'll bring it round this evening, if that's all right.'

'Of course. But I'm speechless.'

'Not totally, I hope.' He took a deep breath. 'I've been wondering: after I go back to Bristol, and you start at Bath, maybe we can go on seeing each other?'

She gasped. 'Are you sure?'

'Positive. You make me feel happy, Hannah.'

'That's how I feel about you too, Ryan.'

He leaned towards her. Their lips were almost touching when Hannah felt something cold and damp, nosing her bare ankle. She looked down to find a small dog on an extending lead grasped by a small boy with a big grin on his face.

'I've brought Toffee to say thank you,' said the lad.

Hannah dropped to her knees and put her arms around the dog.

'Now, isn't that just the icing on the cake?' Ryan whispered.

We do hope that you have enjoyed reading this large print book.

Did you know that all of our titles are available for purchase?

We publish a wide range of high quality large print books including:
**Romances, Mysteries, Classics
General Fiction
Non Fiction and Westerns**

Special interest titles available in large print are:
**The Little Oxford Dictionary
Music Book, Song Book
Hymn Book, Service Book**

Also available from us courtesy of Oxford University Press:
**Young Readers' Dictionary
(large print edition)
Young Readers' Thesaurus
(large print edition)**

For further information or a free brochure, please contact us at:
**Ulverscroft Large Print Books Ltd.,
The Green, Bradgate Road, Anstey,
Leicester, LE7 7FU, England.
Tel:** (00 44) **0116 236 4325**
Fax: (00 44) **0116 234 0205**

CHRISTMAS IN MELTDOWN

Jill Barry

When her assistant suddenly quits, struggling bistro owner Lucy is filled with despair. Top chef James rides to the rescue — but Lucy fears he's hijacking her menus. As electricity fizzes between the two, and festive delights fly from the kitchen, Lucy faces a business dilemma. Does James hold the key to success? Snow poses fresh challenges as each cook falls more deeply in love with the other. Will it be James or Lucy who melts first?

IN PERFECT HARMONY

Wendy Kremer

When Holly Watson starts work as a PA to music director Ian Travers, she's hoping for a simple part-time job to earn a little extra. She gets more than she bargained for, however — her new boss stirs decidedly unprofessional feelings within her. But she's not the only one so affected: Olivia de Noiret, a beautiful and sophisticated prima donna soprano, also has her eyes on Ian — and makes it very clear to Holly that she's already staked her claim . . .

CHRISTMAS IN THE BAY

Jo Bartlett

Maddie Jones runs a bookshop in the beautiful St Nicholas Bay. Devoted to her business, she's forgotten what it's like to have a romantic life — until Ben Cartwright arrives, and reminds her of what she's missing. But Ben isn't being entirely honest about what brings him to town — and when his professional ambition threatens Maddie's livelihood, their relationship seems doomed. When a flash flood descends on the Bay, all the community must pull together — will Ben stay or go?

NOTHING BUT THE BEST

Margaret Sutherland

Natalie's boyfriend Philip is a high-powered, successful surgeon. But while she feels safe and secure in his arms, she resents the way he bottles up his feelings; and how can she challenge him about the long hours he works, when he's doing it to save lives? When Philip discovers that he has inherited a dilapidated seaside cottage from his estranged father, and Natalie must undergo a serious operation, both of them are forced to examine their relationship and decide whether it's likely to stand the test of time.

R.
i.
by